mental_floss

GENIUS INSTRUCTION MANUAL

mental_floss

GENIUS INSTRUCTION MANUAL

edited by Will Pearson, Mangesh
Hattikudur, and John Green

An Imprint of HarperCollinsPublishers

MENTAL_FLOSS: GENIUS INSTRUCTION MANUAL. Copyright
© 2006 by Mental Floss LLC. All rights reserved. Printed in
the United States of America. No part of this book may be
used or reproduced in any manner whatsoever without written permission except in the case of brief quotations embod-
ied in critical articles and reviews. For information, address
HarperCollins Publishers, Inc., 10 East 53rd Street, New
York, NY 10022.

HarperCollins books may be purchased for educational, business, or sales promotional use. For information please write:
Special Markets Department, HarperCollins Publishers, Inc.,
10 East 53rd Street, New York, NY 10022.

FIRST EDITION

Designed by Emily Cavett Taff

Library of Congress Cataloging-in-Publication Data has
been applied for.

ISBN-10: 0-06-088253-0
ISBN-13: 978-0-06-088253-2

---

06 07 08 09 10 WBC/RRD 10 9 8 7 6 5 4 3 2 1

CONTENTS

CONTENTS

CONTENTS

CONTENTS

CONTENTS

PREFACE

A few months ago, the **mental_floss** staff got into a discussion of how we might save the world. But as people who basically only enjoy sitting around and having discussions, we figured we were ill-equipped to—you know—actually *do* anything. We weren't exactly going to cure cancer, or fix poverty, or even build DeLoreans that travel back in time and allow us to save millions of lives by explaining to the year 1931 that, as it turns out, Adolf Hitler would *not* make a very good leader of Germany.

But still, we wanted to make a difference. If we could only save the world, we figured, we could make a lot of money and become very famous. And then, one day, it occurred to us: What this world needs is *more geniuses*. Just look at all the things geniuses have done so far: Tesla and electricity; Newton and physics; Einstein and relativity; Shakespeare and iambic pentameter; Ernest Hemingway and cats (see p. 23). Imagine what a wonderful world we might have if genius were available to everyone! And so we decided to create a single, slim volume that would make its readers brilliantly, searingly smart. Surely this book would change the world for the better. And also sell a lot of copies.

So we called up some geniuses we know and asked them to

write the book. That's when our troubles started. One by one, every Poindexter in our Rolodex refused the task: Stephen Hawking was way too expensive; Bill Gates claimed he had a world to run; Gabriel García Márquez wanted to focus on fiction; Albert Einstein, we were sad to learn, is deceased.

And so it fell to me. I'd like to say that I got the gig because I'm the most brilliant among my colleagues, but I'm afraid the opposite is true: My lack of genius when I began this book was so profound that my job had become insecure. In fact, I was put on genius book duty in the hopes that by taking readers from Normal to Genius, I myself might go on the same journey. And that's precisely what happened to me. A few short months ago, I didn't know my Xeno from my Zero, my fusion from my fission, my *Troilus* and *Love's Labour Lost* from my *Merry Wives of Windsor.* And now, having finished the book, I can tell you with authority: I am still not a genius.

But I can totally fake it. Relativity? No problem. String theory? Check. The ins and outs of major isms? Heck yes. In fact, I know the isms so well that I've created one of my own:

> **geniusishism**
> A difficult-to-pronounce ideology, which holds that feeling like a genius and looking like a genius is about 94% of being a genius.

That is my solemn vow: Careful reading of this book will either make you a genius, or else it will make you geniusish, which according to my calculations is basically just as good. So, go ahead and dive in. The brilliant topics enclosed should have your mind bouncing around like a giant genius pinball, hitting one unpredictable revelation after another. After all, what does your understanding of teleporting have to do with the romantic strategies of various eggheads? And what's *that* got to do with the intricacies and efficacies of various genius dress codes? Nothing, except you're going to be a whole lot smarter after this wild ride, so buckle up and enjoy it. And while you're at it, tell your friends to enjoy it. And also, their friends. Because the world needs saving, cancer needs curing, climate change needs addressing, and quantum mechanics needs refining. And you, future genius, are just the person for the job.

STARTING OFF LIGHT: HOBBIES AND EXTRA-CURRICULAR ACTIVITIES YOU MIGHT WANT TO TAKE UP

(If you're serious about this whole Genius Thing)

Chess

Although genius chess players occasionally suffer from some problems (noted chess master Bobby Fischer, for example, had all the silver fillings in his teeth removed so the KGB would stop transmitting radio signals through them), quite a lot of geniuses have enjoyed chess, including:

Early in his career filmmaker **Stanley Kubrick**, supplemented his income largely by hustling chess players in New York's Washington Square.

Ludwig van Beethoven, a chess fanatic who was friends with the man who invented the Turk, the world's first chess automaton. A cupboard-shaped contraption that appeared to be a robot but was actually controlled by a skilled player hiding inside it, the Turk beat many of the greatest luminaries of the 18th century, from Napoleon to . . .

Benjamin Franklin, who once said, "The game of chess is not merely an idle amusement . . . for life is a kind of chess."

Play an Instrument

Not all geniuses go in for music, of course. **Samuel Johnson** was once told that a particular violin piece was very difficult. "Difficult, do you call it, Sir?" Johnson replied. "I wish it were impossible." But the irascible Dr. Johnson aside, a great many geniuses played an instrument in their spare time, including:

Beginning when he was about 6 and ending when he was 13, **Albert Einstein** took violin lessons. A lot of us can say that, of course, but Einstein actually stuck with the instrument, and enjoyed playing at parties well into his old age. You've never partied until you've partied with physicists. Their partying force (f) equals the mass (m) of bodies on the dance floor times the acceleration (a) of the DJ's beats, if you know what we're saying. (For the record, we don't really know what we're saying.)

Benjamin Franklin, who, it is quickly becoming clear, found time to do *everything*. Franklin played the viola and also invented an instrument he called the glass armonica, which produces music in much the same manner as rubbing a wet finger on a wine glass.

Before he became chairman of the Federal Reserve and was acclaimed for his brilliant economics mind, **Alan Greenspan** was a professional jazz musician, playing saxophone and clarinet in jazz clubs in New York's Greenwich Village in the 1950s. In fact, Greenspan attended the world-renowned Julliard School before getting a Bachelor of Science degree from NYU's School of Commerce.

Drinking

Now, we're not going to *advise* that you drink. Drinking can be very bad for geniuses (witness the poet Dylan Thomas, who died at the tender age of 39 soon after noting: "I've had eighteen straight whiskeys; I believe that's the record"). We're just saying that quite a lot of people who enjoy a good drink seem to end up geniuses, including:

Noted comic genius and part-time philosopher W. C. Fields said, "A man's got to believe in something. I believe I'll have another drink."

It's probably no coincidence that **Tennessee Williams** wrote so brilliantly about alcoholics (see, for instance, the character Brick in *Cat on a Hot Tin Roof*). A lifelong alcoholic who wrote all of his plays while drinking, Williams liked to work early in the morning, and usually had his first martini down by 8 A.M.

Widely considered the best dancer of her era, **Isadora Duncan** (1878–1927) was known for her long string of love affairs and for her absolute inability not to spend money the moment it was given her. Being perpetually short of cash and an alcoholic tends to lead to poor decisions: According to her biographer, Duncan sometimes mixed cologne with the last dregs of various wine bottles to cop a buzz. So if anybody ever offers you a cocktail called "The Isadora," you're well advised to pass.

HOBBIES AND EXTRA-CURRICULAR ACTIVITIES YOU MIGHT WANT TO AVOID

Sports

Those seeking the bright lights of political genius might be well-advised to play sports (Teddy Roosevelt was a boxer; Gerald Ford an all-American football player; George W. Bush a cheerleader at Andover), but your standard geniuses tend to be miserable at sports. Nuclear physicist **Robert Oppenheimer**, for instance, was so embarrassed by his lack of physical fitness that not only did he opt out of sports as a child, he also refused to climb stairs at his school. Man, if only Robert Oppenheimer had been in school with us, we might not have been picked last for kickball.

Opium

So how come drinking made the list of hobbies to acquire and opium's stuck on habits to avoid? Maybe it's because while drinking kills you and everything, it doesn't nip your genius in the bud quite like opium tends to.

You might argue that **Samuel Taylor Coleridge** benefited from opium, since his masterful, but unfinished, "Kubla Khan" was originally conceived during an opium dream. But Coleridge lost decades of potential productivity to the drug. He rarely left

4

his house, was perennially near suicide, and couldn't finish a poem to save his life.

If you need further proof, just consider that there was only one way to be a Brontë sibling and *not* succeed: Opium. **Branwell Brontë**, the ne'er do well brother of Anne, Charlotte, and Emily, was a promising young poet until he became irrevocably addicted to opium. (Fans of the young Branwell's writing included none other than the aforementioned S. T. Coleridge.)

While there's no record that **Sigmund Freud** ever smoked or ate opium, it's well established that he used the opiate cocaine on many occasions. Back in the good ole days of psychology, when psychologists intentionally gave their patients malaria to treat syphilis and jammed ice picks into the eye sockets of people suffering hysteria, cocaine was regularly prescribed as "a euphoric." In fact, Freud's "research" into cocaine led him to prescribe the drug to a friend addicted to morphine. It didn't work: The friend merely

Catching Tuberculosis

Probably the number-one pastime of geniuses throughout history has been "getting tuberculosis." Maybe it's because geniuses tend to congregate together and tuberculosis is easily transmitted through coughing and sneezing. Or maybe it's just that geniuses tend to be a bit less robust than most of us. Regardless, budding geniuses such as you should be particularly grateful that most strains of TB can be effectively treated with antibiotics. Examples of the brilliant and tubercular include Paul Gauguin, Mozart, Alexander Graham Bell, and Frederic Chopin.

Oh, and also pretty much every 19th-century writer. Seriously: Elizabeth Barrett Browning, Lord Byron, Anton Chekov, Stephen Crane, Fyodor Dostoyevsky, Ralph Waldo Emerson, Percy Bysshe Shelley, Franz Kafka, John Keats, Edgar Allan Poe, Robert Louis Stevenson, Henry David Thoreau, Jane Austen, and all five Brontë sisters.

switched addictions to cocaine, (which eventually proved fatal *and he died any way*).

Although she's mostly famous for the children's book *Little Women*, **Louisa May Alcott**'s novel *Work* features a female protagonist addicted to opium eating and gambling. Alcott lived by the maxim that you should write what you know—she herself was addicted to the opiate laudanum.

Alchemy

Although it's no longer in fashion, seeking a way to turn lead into gold used to be *the* way for geniuses to pass their lazy Sunday afternoons. And boy, was it a bad idea. Aside from the risks posed by soaking toxic lead in a series of randomly selected toxic chemicals, alchemy took valuable time away from the *real* work of such geniuses as Isaac "Gravity" Newton, Thomas "Catholicism's Greatest Theologian" Aquinas, and Robert "Despite my funny last name I managed to become the first modern chemist" Boyle.

14 SENTENCES ABOUT 14 SHAKESPEARE COMEDIES

And now for something lighthearted and fun. Shipwrecks, traitors, rape—that sort of stuff. Okay, so Shakespeare's comedies aren't always funny. But they're generally less bloody than his histories and tragedies. Although the bard's reputation rests largely on the brooding stuff (the *Macbeths* and *Hamlets*), you'll need to know the comedies if you truly want to impress with your obscure knowledge. And, let's face it, every genius needs some familiarity with the undisputed heavyweight champ of literature. Not long after Shaekspeare's death in 1616, Ben Jonson wrote, "He was not of an age, but for all time!" Indeed, lunchtime, dinnertime, downtime, even naptime (for all our aspiring preschool geniuses trying to make a good impression); sprinkling in a little Shakespeare always goes a long way. And so:

The Comedies

A Midsummer Night's Dream: Complicated interconnected plots don't lend themselves to single-sentence summaries, but basically this girl Hermia and her boyfriend Lysander try to elope while fairy king Oberon and his estranged fairy wife fight and a bunch of low-rent traveling actors rehearse a play, and then eventually everyone lives happily ever after despite a brief scare, when Oberon's wife falls in love with a guy with a donkey head.

All's Well That Ends Well: Helena, who's gorgeous but from a low-rent family, gets to marry her dream man, Count Bertram, who enjoys her company so little that he immediately heads off to war, desperately hoping he'll die before he has to return to Helena; but Bertram ends up not dying, making the play one that ends happily, but doesn't end particularly well (*AWTEW* is one of Shakespeare's least-regarded plays.)

As You Like It: A duke (who's never given a proper name) is unseated from his duchy, whereupon he moves to the forest for a while until the duke's traitorous son is saved from a lioness by the duke's loyal servant, which leads to no fewer than *four* weddings, and the duke's return to dukeness.

Cymbeline: So poorly regarded that some scholars think Shakespeare wrote it as a joke, *Cymbeline* stars Posthumus (that's his name), who gets kicked out of a kingdom for secretly marrying the king's daughter, which leads to a series of events so convoluted that in Act V, Scene IV, the god Jupiter descends from heaven and orders everyone to shut up and explain what's going on, which everyone does, whereupon the play ends with no deaths, making it a comedy.

Love's Labour Lost: Three men who've *just* sworn off girls happen across three attendants to a beautiful princess, and sure enough they forget their swears.

Measure for Measure: A favorite in political science classes, a politico named Angelo condemns young Claudio to death for getting his fiancée pregnant, but then Angelo, in a stirringly honorable turn, agrees to spare Claudio's fornication if Angelo can engage in some fornication of his own with Claudio's hot sister—an event that is narrowly averted, perhaps because it would have been hard to stage, what with everybody being played by guys.

The Merchant of Venice: Classified as a comedy, even though its most famous character, the Jewish moneylender Shylock, ends up bankrupt after trying to extract a pound of flesh from Antonio, who is saved by the lawyer-like contract analysis of the hot young heiress Portia (who's like Paris Hilton, except smart).

The Merry Wives of Windsor: Sir John Falstaff tries to win over two wealthy, married Windsor women—and fails, making him, perhaps, the stage's first fat, ugly guy who can't get lucky (cf. George Costanza).

Much Ado About Nothing: The romantic comedy that's been copied by every romantic comedy that ever starred Hugh Grant and/or Julia Roberts: A guy (Benedick) leaves his fiancée (Hero) at the altar and, after a series of miscommunications, ends up marrying his true love, Beatrice (which is a lovely story, unless you happen to be Hero).

Pericles, Prince of Tyre: Shakespeare probably only wrote the last 13 scenes (everything before is pretty wretched) of this play that follows the seafaring adventures of the title character, who faces a lot of impediments (a shipwreck, pirates, and a girl with a *serious* Electra complex) before he finally manages to get married.

The Taming of the Shrew: A vulgar, man-hating shrew, Katherina Minola, is (eventually) tamed by her suitor, Petruccio, but not before Shakespeare reveals a hint of misogyny.

Terms Shakespeare Coined

Full circle
Foregone conclusion
Brave new world
Bated breath
Neither rhyme nor reason
Strange bedfellows
A spotless reputation
Method in the madness
Arch-villain
Well-bred

The Comedy of Errors: Shakespeare's shortest play, and our shortest summary: Egeon almost loses his life, his wife, and his children—but then doesn't.

The Tempest: In the greatest of Shakespeare's later plays, the sorcerer Prospero and his daughter Miranda are stranded on an island with the deformed (and possibly homosexual) Caliban, when a second shipwreck brings ashore the man of Miranda's dreams.

Twelfth Night: This cross-dressing, gender-bending extravaganza stars Viola (a girl) who lives as Cesario (a boy), who works for Duke Orsino (a boy), who's in love with Olivia (a girl), who herself falls in love with Viola/Cesario (a, uh, whatever), who's in love with the duke, and it only gets more complicated from there until finally the duke marries Viola and Olivia marries Viola's brother Sebastian (who, we forgot to mention, washes ashore after a shipwreck round about Act II).

The Two Gentlemen of Verona: Two gentlemen from Verona find—you'll never guess—love, although in this case it's after a discomfiting, pathos-ridden scene in which one of the purported "gentlemen" attempts to rape the character Silvia.

The Two Noble Kinsmen: This tragicomedy often lumped with Shakespeare's comedies was a collaboration with lesser playwright John Fletcher in which two cousins fight over a princess;

eventually, the cousin who hasn't just died (Palamon) gets to marry the princess.

The Winter's Tale: Set in Bohemia, this play features a character named Hermione (see also, Harry Potter), the oracle of Delphi, a magical resurrection, and Shakespeare's most famous stage direction: *Exit, pursued by a bear.*

TELEPORTATION

Although it pains our tribble-shaped Trekkie hearts, we're going to get through this entire discussion of the actual science behind teleportation without a single mention of *Star Trek*, because teleportation isn't just for science fiction anymore.

The word "teleportation" was coined at the beginning of the 20th century by writer Charles Fort to describe inexplicable appearances and disappearances, such as—honestly—the disappearance of socks from the dryer. By the 1930s, teleportation had its current meaning: moving stuff from one place to another almost instantaneously. The concept has been around in various forms longer than that. Many Christian saints are said to have had some kind of teleportation powers, including Philip the Baptist, who in chapter 8 of Acts instantaneously travels from the desert near Gaza to Azotus, a journey of almost 25 miles.

But the craziest thing about teleportation is that, at least on the atomic level, it actually seems to be possible. In the early 1990s, a group of scientists argued that what we know about quantum physics, or the physics and behavior of minute specks of energy and matter on the atomic and subatomic level, makes teleportation possible, and that it could be instantaneous.

The idea is to circumvent the general rule that nothing in the universe travels faster than light by using a phenomenon called entanglement. Entanglement is complicated, but basically: If you prepare two quantum systems together, they'll remain entangled even if separated, and that entanglement allows for nearly instantaneous movement between the two systems. In quantum teleportation, the original matter is destroyed in the first system and then immediately and exactly re-created in the other system. This poses some problems for human teleportation, because if you are killed in one place and then reformed in another place as a result of quantum teleportation, are you still alive? And are you still yourself? No one knows, and we're certainly not gonna volunteer for the job.

Today scientists can transfer the characteristics of matter, but not the matter itself. The first successful teleportation involved the quantum teleportation of photons in 2002. A team of Australian scientists used entanglement to teleport a laser beam the remarkable distance of *one entire meter*. Still, *you* try magically moving billions of photons instantaneously. More recently, two separate teams of scientists have successfully teleported an ion from one quantum system to another (again, across a relatively short distance).

The feasibility of quantum teleportation again shows the mind-boggling weirdness of quantum mechanics, certainly, but it may not have many practical uses in the short run. At this point, it takes a tremendous amount of work to transfer the properties of a single ionized atom from one end of a well-equipped laboratory to the other. Successfully teleporting a human would involve the transfer of about 7,000,000,000,000,000,000,000,000,000 atoms. Also, teleporting a person's atoms in the exact right order to the exact right place may prove to be a challenge because of Heisenberg's Uncertainty Principle (see p. 139).

Bilocation

It's not quite teleportation, but it's close. Bilocation, the ability to be in two places at the same time, is a surprisingly common talent in Catholic saints, and not just in the old days: Italian priest Padre Pio (1887–1968) was said to have powers of bilocation. According to the Church, he once appeared in the air over a small Italian town during World War II to stop Americans from bombing the city.

In short, that's a long way off—if it's even possible. Nonetheless, quantum teleportation may prove to have significant implications. In 2004, scientists teleported the "quantum states" of light particles more than 2,000 feet, and some scientists believe that the teleportation of bits of information through entanglement, which is known as "quantum communication," could change the way computers work, allowing processors to run almost infinitely fast. Now if we could only build some Phasers. (Sorry—we tried.)

10%

genius

Congratulations! You are now 10% of the way toward full-fledged Genius.

Now, we don't wish to belittle your accomplishment, but you've still got a ways to go before you become a full-fledged genius. At this point, your genius level is approximately comparable to that of the late 19th-century inventor of the first vacuum cleaner–like device, whose name—for reasons that will soon become clear—has been lost to history. The inventor created a primitive blowing machine that blew pressurized air onto carpets—in the vague hope that the newly airborne dust would land in an open bag on top of the apparatus. This involved quite a lot of deft maneuvering on the inventor's part, but, it also stirred up more dust than it cleaned—although, as we'll see later, the blowing vacuum led directly to a significant innovation.

RELATIVITY

Unfortunately, the only way to *fully* understand the discovery that changed the course of Einstein's two theories of relativity is to learn a lot of math, specifically something called "tensor calculus." Fortunately for you, we aren't going to attempt to teach you tensor calculus, mostly because we don't understand it. Also, tensor calculus is not important to the actual theme of Einsteinian relativity, which is: "Man, this universe is really, really weird."

Contrary to popular belief, Einstein did not discover relativity as an idea. Galileo stumbled across it, as did Newton, hence Newtonian physics. Take the "*two* trains passing each other" example. Brad Pitt is on one train; Angelina Jolie is on another. If those trains travel together in the same direction at the same speed, we know two things:

1. Billy Bob Thornton is probably on the roof of one of those trains, and he's mad.

2. Relative to each other, the two trains are not moving. Had they known about celebrity-packed trains, Galileo and Newton would have argued that the trains' speed cannot be measured against each other;

it can only be measured relative to the earth (which is also moving, and whose movement can only be measured relative to another system). But this classical theory of relativity presupposes that the laws of mechanics are the same everywhere, and that space and time are independent realities.

But in the 19th century, people started to notice that while this seemed like a fine idea, it did not actually work. When, for instance, physicists attempted to measure the earth's movement through space the way they would measure a ship's movement through the ocean, the answers came out all wrong, which caused a lot of physicists to twist their hair in confusion.

In the end, it was the guy who had the most hair to twist, Albert Einstein, who solved the conundrum, and in doing so, completely upended our understanding of the world. In physics, 1905 is known as the *Annus Mirabilis*, "The Year of Wonders." And for good reason: Einstein published three hugely important papers. The first proved the existence of the energy bundles we now called photons; the second proved the actual existence of atoms (based on Brownian motion); and the third, with the gripping title "On the Electrodynamics of Moving Bodies," introduced the special theory of relativity.

In that paper, Einstein argued that the speed of light (aka c) is invariant. This is where you might just choose not to believe us because it doesn't make any sense unless you understand tensor calculus, but: The speed of light, which is also—*Star Trek* aside—probably the fastest speed possible—is constant for all observers. If I am standing still and you are flying an F-16 at MACH-3, we both perceive light to be traveling at the same speed, about 300,000,000 meters per second.

Space-Time Continuum

Shortly after Einstein published his theory of special relativity, Hermann Minkowski used it to show that space and time are not, as everyone had always believed, absolutely independent of each other, but are rather parts of a whole.

To prove this, let's begin with President Abraham Lincoln. Lincoln was six feet four inches tall, right? It doesn't matter where he's located when you measure him, or whether you use measuring tape or a really long ruler, or when in his life you—wait. It *does* matter when you measure him, because on February 13, 1809, Lincoln wasn't even close to six feet four inches tall, on account of how he was one day old. So when you're trying to measure the length of Abraham Lincoln, time matters.

This, as it turns out, is true not only of Abraham Lincoln but also of everything else in the universe. Besides moving

This may not seem like a particularly earth-shattering revelation, but it was. For one thing, the theory of special relativity implied that mass and energy are interchangeable, which suggested the possibility of nuclear fission, which in turn led to two bombs, the end of World War II, and the deaths of 200,000 people. Special relativity also showed that the rate of a moving clock appears to decrease as speed increases (see the sidebar for an explanation of that weirdness), that events that appear simultaneous to you may not appear simultaneous to someone in a different system, and that absolute time cannot be measured (which, among other implications, means that theoretically an Olympic track and field athlete could challenge her results due to the impossibility of measuring absolute time).

A decade later, Einstein proposed his General Theory of Relativity, which, to further confuse matters, is much more specialized and generally less general than special relativity. General relativity involves the acceleration of objects, and holds that the presence of matter (like the earth, or Abraham Lincoln) causes curvature of space-time, as shown in this picture:

through three-dimensional space, we are also moving through time. In short, space and time are not absolute, independent realities. They are part of the same continuum, cleverly known as the space-time continuum.

Whereas classical physics ascribed the movement of bodies (like the orbit of a planet) to the force of gravity, general relativity ascribes such movement to inertial motion resulting from the curves in space-time. For example, general relativity accounts for the highly eccentric orbit of Mercury in a way that gravitational theory cannot.

General relativity also accounts for the fact that, instead of falling off the bottom of the earth into the vacuum of space, people in Australia tend to be just fine. While we perceive this as being the result of the force of gravity, general relativity holds that we don't freefall off the earth due to continuous physical acceleration. You may not *feel* like you are constantly accelerating, but you are, due to the mechanical resistance of the earth. This has implications of its own. For instance, the fact that we are constantly accelerating seems to us like a good enough workout; in the face of never-ending acceleration, jogging seems a little ridiculous.

THE GENIUS
GUIDE TO
ACQUIRING PETS

In order to truly attain geniusishness, you'll need to let genius seep into every corner of your life, including pet ownership. What, you don't think the right pet will help you become a genius? Frederic Chopin, as you'll see below, would beg to differ.

Like many introverts, **Isaac Newton** got along better with pets than he did with people. His dog, Diamond, was one of his best friends—although legend has it that Diamond caused Newton to have a nervous breakdown. Running around one day, Diamond knocked over a candle, causing a fire that destroyed many of Newton's manuscripts and twenty years' worth of calculations. After despairing, "O Diamond! O Diamond! Thou little knowest what mischief than hast done!" Newton sank into a deep depression.

But perhaps the most famous story of Newton's pets may be apocryphal: Although he is often credited with inventing the cat flap to allow his felines free access in and out of the house, there's no hard evidence that he actually did. However, Newton did invent calculus—so cut him some slack.

Elizabeth Barrett Browning's cocker spaniel, Flush, was the subject of a biography written by no less a literary genius than Virginia Woolf. *Flush* is probably Woolf's least-admired book, although in 1933 the *New York Times* called it "a brilliant biographical tour-de-force." (This of a book that devotes pages to the joys of eating pudding.) Remarkably, Flush (the dog) also starred in *another* book, as well as a play.

Purportedly, **George Eliot** spent almost her entire book advance buying her pug, Pug. For that kind of money, you'd think she might have given him, like, a real name. But she clearly fancied her cleverness: A pug named Pug makes an appearance in her novel *Adam Bede*.

Lexicographer, wit, and all-around genius **Samuel Johnson** loved his cat, Hodge, so much that he would make daily trips to the market to ensure Hodge ate only the freshest oysters. Johnson's biographer, James Boswell, immortalized Johnson's description of Hodge as "a very fine cat indeed." After Hodge's death, the poet Percival Stockdale—they don't make names like that anymore—wrote "An Elegy on the Death of Dr. Johnson's Favourite Cat."

Legend has it that **Frédéric Chopin** was inspired to write his "Waltz No. 4 in F Major" after hearing his cat walk across his piano. Later, **F. Scott Fitzgerald** had a cat named Chopin, who is not recorded to have inspired anything.

If you want to be a genius, you'll do well to name your pet after another genius. It worked for Fitzgerald, and also for first lady of feminism, **Gloria Steinem**, who owned a cat named Magritte.

It's always nice to have someone in your house who not only loves you but believes in your genius. So take a lesson from **Paul Cézanne**, who taught his pet parrot to say, "Cézanne is a great painter!"

Lord Byron is most famous for having an extraordinarily long list of paramours. Oh, and also his poetry. But few know that he was known to travel with five cats, including one named

Beppo. Clearly, ladies love men who love cats. Which is a lesson that **Ernest Hemingway** must have taken to heart, because Hemingway—for all his reputation as a bull-fightin', swashbucklin', gun-shootin' macho man—was something of a crazy cat lady. He had about 30 cats in all (with names like Boise, Crazy Christian, and Fats). Many of his cats had six toes on each paw, which is why cats with extra toes, known technically as polydactyls, are often called "Hemingway cats."

T. S. Eliot was so fond of cats that the genius known for such dense modernist works as *The Wasteland* was inspired by his band of cats to write a book of light-hearted verse about the feline mind called *Old Possum's Book of Practical Cats*. That was all fine and good until 1981, when a decided non-genius named Richard Stilgoe and his friend Andrew Lloyd Webber decided to turn the book into a musical, *CATS*, which spent two decades on Broadway in spite of its being, in retrospect, embarrassingly awful.

The Ancient Greek poet **Virgil** once had a lavish funeral for a common housefly he claimed was his pet. Virgil wrote several poems for the fly, hired an orchestra to play, paid mourners to weep for it, and had a special mausoleum built for the fly. In short, Virgil was crazy—like a fox. The Greek

Even Really Horrible Tycoons Love Their Dogs

Oil baron J. Paul Getty was in Europe when his 12-year-old son died of a brain tumor. Being the sort of kind and loving father you'd expect a ruthless oil baron to be, Getty did not return from his trip for young Timmy's funeral. His diary that day read, "Funeral. Sad day. Amoco up 2 and 7/8ths, Gulf down 1 and 3/4." But when his dog died of cancer just a few years later, Getty reportedly wept for three straight days.

And in the, Uh, Okay Category:

The French symbolist poet Gérard de Nerval had a series of nervous breakdowns and eventually committed suicide, but before mental illness completely took over his life, de Nerval owned a pet lobster, which he would take for walks around Paris, using a length of blue ribbon as a leash. The advantages to lobsters as pets? According to de Nerval, they are "peaceful, serious creatures, who know the secrets of the sea, and do not bark."

government was planning to parcel rich people's land out to war veterans. The only exception was land that contained "burial plots," which—post–fly funeral—Virgil's estate could claim.

Dorothy Parker reportedly briefly owned a pair of baby alligators. Parker's maid quit immediately upon finding the gators in Parker's bathtub, leaving a note reading: "Dear Madam, I am leaving, as I cannot work in a house with alligators. I would have told you this before, but I never thought the subject would come up."

BUILDING A NETWORK: FAMOUS GROUPS OF GENIUSES

In some ways, genius is a lot like collegiate popularity: You may acquire it on your own by sheer force of will and wit, or you can just join a really prestigious sorority. After all, a good network of geniuses can save its lesser members from historical obscurity. Unfortunately, none of the groups below exist anymore, so your best bet is getting together with other readers of this book, and forming small genius groups. In short, you need to start living *The Genius-Driven Life*.

Algonquin Round Table

What It Was: Beginning in 1919, a group of men and women of letters met every weekday for lunch at the Algonquin Hotel in New York City. The only table that could accommodate the dozen or more people who showed up daily? Why, a large, round one, of course—hence the name. The stars of the Round Table were poet Dorothy Parker, playwright Edna Ferber, playwright George S. Kaufman, and comedian Harpo Marx. Many legendary quips were made at the Round Table—one of our favorite involves the notoriously taciturn Calvin Coolidge. When another Round Tablean informed Dorothy Parker that Coolidge had died, Parker responded, "How can they tell?" The Round Table lunches lasted into the early 1930s—although even after they went their separate ways, its members were always remembered for their association with it. (Just like Judd Nelson and the Brat Pack.)

Who It Saved from Obscurity: *New Yorker* writer and wit Alexander Woollcott, who in his day was as famous as James Thurber, but might be entirely forgotten by most people were it not for his prominent place in the Algonquin Round Table. Woollcott ought to be more famous, because he was hilarious. He once quipped that fellow Round Tablean Harold Ross, his boss at the *New Yorker*, looked "like a dishonest Abe Lincoln." He also called Los Angeles "seven suburbs in search of a city."

Bloomsbury Group

What It Was: The Bloomsbury Group (or Bloomsbury Set) was sort of the Algonquin Round Table of Britain, except it lasted longer (from about 1907 to 1930) and, if anything, contained more famous people. Its core members included the novelist Virginia Woolf, the hugely important economist John Maynard Keynes, and E. M. Forster, the author of *Howard's End*. While hanging out at the Algonquin mostly meant cracking jokes, the Bloomsbury Group was serious about their work: At Virginia's house in London's Bloomsbury section, they studied aesthetics and philosophy together, seeking better definitions of words like "good" and "true." In early 20th-century London, *everyone* wanted to hang out with the Bloomsburians: Visitors to their meetings included Bertrand Russell, T. S. Eliot, and Aldous Huxley—all of who agreed with the Bloomsburians about refusing to accept traditional morality and value judgments.

Who It Saved from Obscurity: Plenty of people, but perhaps most notably Lytton Strachey, who wrote a few biographies and nothing else, and yet has an entry in the *Encyclopedia Britannica*, which is better than we're doing.

The Oxford Experimental Philosophy Club

What It Was: It sounds like the world's lamest club. Maybe so, but you'd have been hard-pressed to get into it, with members like John Locke (who is still read in political sciences classes), Robert Boyle (for whom chemistry's "Boyle's Law" is named), Robert Hooke (who invented the microscope), and Christopher Wren (the architect for London's St. Paul's cathedral). In the mid-17th century, all these men were in and around Oxford, England, and their "club" often met at Boyle's house to chat about how fun it was to be a genius. They also spent a lot of time with human carcasses, cutting them open in an attempt to better understand the workings of the body.

Saved from Obscurity: Thomas Willis, a country doctor who ended up getting to hang out with the Experimental Philosophy Club as a kind of mascot (if the Oxford club was "Our Gang," Willis was Alfalfa). Willis ended up becoming moderately well-remembered for a series of important discoveries about the brain—none of which he would have made without his boys in Oxford.

HOW TO DRESS LIKE A RIGHT-BRAINED GENIUS

James Joyce, John Lennon, Gandhi, Michael Jackson (calling him a genius is a stretch, admittedly, but *Thriller* was really good). A good pair of glasses just plain makes you look geniusier, which perhaps explains why Britney Spears sometimes wears them—despite her reportedly perfect vision.

Many recent studies have claimed that "major depressive disorder" is between 8 and 10 times more common in writers and artists than in regular people, so if you really want to dress like a right-brained genius, you need to turn that grin upside down. Many psychologists believe that depression is caused not by creativity itself, but by the artist's tendency toward endless self-reflection.

Just check out the list of right-brained geniuses who puffed on pipes: French deconstructionist Jacques Derrida, J.R.R. Tolkien, Vincent van Gogh, Mr. Potato Head. (Okay, Mr. Potato Head was not a genius, but he did smoke a pipe until 1987.) What do all these people have in common? Besides Mr. Potato Head, who, as we mentioned, quit, they're all dead, which is why we advise the bubble pipe instead of the smoking kind.

You're a genius, remember. You don't need no stinking *hairbrush*. From Van Gogh to Mark Twain to Einstein, messy hair is a staple of geniuses, whether right-brained or not.

Right-brained geniuses of old tended to wear cheap suits. As people with strong aesthetic senses, right-brained geniuses want to look good. But they're generally poorer than their left-brained counterparts (even geniuses successful in their lifetime, like Beethoven and William Faulkner, always fretted about money). So hit the thrift store for your clothes, but stick to the suit aisle. No more ironic T-shirts or pre-ripped blue jeans, if you're serious about being a genius.

RICH GENIUS, POOR GENIUS: SOME FINANCIAL DOS AND DON'TS FROM THE ANNALS OF GENIUSIA

DO: Patent your work. Aside from costing yourself money, failure to patent will cost you fame. Thomas Edison is immortalized in the research projects of fourth graders everywhere as America's greatest inventor. And, indeed, Edison held more patents (1,093) than anyone in American history. But patenting everything was part of his genius. You never read little-kid papers about Nikola Tesla, who was probably the more important scientist but who rarely patented his work. Indeed, Edison borrowed (and promptly patented) several of Tesla's innovations in electricity.

DON'T: Spend all your money on drugs. This seems like reasonably obvious advice, but historically, geniuses have a pretty spotty record when it comes to investing their fortunes in a product that will simultaneously bankrupt and kill them. From Billie Holiday, who for the last years of her life was forbidden from performing in New York jazz clubs because of her heroin abuse, to Stephen King, who doesn't remember "a couple of books" he wrote due to cocaine, there are better ways to spend your money. Like . . .

DO: Start your own publishing company. Well, if you're a brilliant writer, anyway. In a decade of business, Mark Twain's publishing house, the Charles L. Webster Company, managed to publish what might be America's greatest novel (*The Adventures of Huckleberry Finn*) and what is unquestionably America's greatest presidential memoir (*Personal Recollections of Ulysses S. Grant*). The company was successful despite Twain's utter lack of business acumen, although it did eventually go bankrupt in 1894, which reminds us . . .

DON'T: Let an incompetent friend of the family run your publishing company.

DO: Acquire a loyal patron, preferably a pope. Even better, seven popes, as Michelangelo managed to do, on account of how he lived in an era where the average Pope lived about eight weeks. The patronage business strategy worked particularly well for Renaissance artists and classical composers, but it's worth at least trying to revive.

DON'T: Give your technology-related product a human name. Not only does this tend to work

DON'T:

Invent anything having to do with a television.

It's hard to imagine where we'd be without the founding fathers of television. "Couch potato" would not exist as a phrase; those of us unhappy with real presidents wouldn't be able to watch the antics of fake ones; and Charlie Sheen's career could never have been revived. But for all the scientific pioneers of television gave us, most of them ended up worse off, both financially and personally. Most notably:

Lee de Forest, who ushered in the electronic age by inventing a vacuum tube that amplified electronic signals, spent his fortune suing other patent holders, and started a series of failed companies. On the personal side, he was married four times and arrested for mail fraud.

Philo T. Farnsworth, who first drew designs for a

television when he was 14 and successfully developed the first working one when he was just 21, and—well, that was about it for the good news. Farnsworth never felt he got the credit he deserved, and he was too busy smoking and drinking himself to death to try to invent anything else.

out poorly in the movies (see, for instance, the fate of HAL 9000 in *2010: Odyssey 2*), it also has a terrible track record in real life. Two of the great technological geniuses of our time have made this mistake: Microsoft's Bill Gates and Apple's Steve Jobs. In 1983, Apple computer released the Lisa, the first computer with a graphical interface. That was really cool and all, but no one in 1983 wanted to pay $10,000 for a computer, partly because only about 16 people in 1983 knew what a computer was. The project was a financial disaster for Apple, and marked the beginning of the PC's dominance in the workplace.

In 1995, Microsoft released BOB, a user interface that was supposed to make Windows 3.1 hip and cool. But computer programmers, as it turned out, don't know from cool: The product bombed. But it wasn't a total loss for Bill Gates: The project manager for Bob, Melinda French, later became his wife.

DO: Try to win the Nobel Prize, or at least share one. Aside from the sheer joy of calling yourself a Nobel laureate, the lucrative speaking engagements, and a gold medal big enough to make Mr. T jealous, each prize comes with a cash bonus—around $1.3 million in 2006.

20%

genius

Congratulations! You are now 20% of the way toward full-fledged Genius.

You've definitely made some progress. The way we figure it, your genius is now comparable to British engineer Hubert Cecil Booth. You might recall that earlier, you were at the level of the nameless inventor of the Amazing Dust-Blowing Machine. Well, turns out that Hubert saw an exhibition of that very machine blowing air onto carpets in a vain attempt to dust them. When Booth asked the ne'er-do-well inventor why his machine blew instead of sucking, the inventor insisted that sucking was impossible. Booth reportedly then knelt down, put his mouth to a plush chair, and sucked on it—whereupon he very nearly choked to death, because back in the late 19th century, they hadn't vacuumed in, like, *forever*. Fortunately Booth survived, and in 1901, he invented the first vacuum cleaner to work via sucking rather than blowing. We're doing our very best not to note the gajillion double entendres here, but we do feel compelled to share that Booth only made matters worse by naming his first machine the Puffing Billy.

A CONFEDERACY OF DUNCES: THE BUSINESS & SCIENCE EDITION

Jonathan Swift once wrote, "When a true genius appears in the world, you may know him by this sign, that the dunces are all in confederacy against him." So feel no trepidation when people in high places start saying that your brilliant ideas are nuts. People in high places are often wrong:

Ken Olsen, the cofounder of the Digital Equipment Company, famously said in 1977, "There is no reason for any individual to have a computer in his home." The quote, as it turns out, is taken slightly out of context—he meant people wouldn't want a *Jetsons*-style mainframe running their houses. (Although, boy, would we!) But a decade later, Olsen clearly hadn't learned his lesson, earning the enmity of computer geeks everywhere by saying, "Unix is snake oil." Unix, an operating system whose demise is oft-lamented, is a distant cousin of today's geek-friendly open-source Linux operating system.

In an 1876 internal memo (who knew there were internal memos back then?), telegraph company **Western Union** wrote, "The telephone has too many shortcomings to be seriously considered as a means of communication. The device is inherently of no value to us." As fate would have it, the *telegram* had the shortcomings: Western Union STOP discontinued telegram service STOP on January 27, 2006, meaning that future generations of readers STOP won't even get this joke STOP

Although Scots-Irish physicist **Lord Kelvin** was a genius and a baron, and although he got a temperature scale named after him, he had awful luck predicting the future. He wrongly believed in an unbreakable solid atom and so refused to acknowledge the possibility of a nuclear chain reaction. His other huge gaffe? In 1895, he said, "Heavier-than-air flying machines are impossible." Just eight years later, the Wright brothers proved him wrong.

Lee de Forest, who patented the vacuum tube that helped make television, radio, and computers possible, once said, "While theoretically and technically television may be feasible, commercially and financially it is an impossibility."

Before they started their own company to sell their home computers, **Steve Jobs** and **Steve Wozniak** tried desperately to sell their product to a bigger company. To quote Jobs: "So we went to Atari and said, 'Hey, we've got this amazing thing, even built with some of your parts, and what do you think about funding us? Or we'll give it to you. We just want to do it. Pay our salary, we'll come work for you.' And they said, 'No.' So then we went to Hewlett-Packard, and they said, 'Hey, we don't need you. You haven't got through college yet.'" Instead, Jobs and Wozniak started Apple Computer—where, admittedly, they'd make some confederacy-of-dunces-type blunders of their own.

"The concept is interesting and well-formed, but in order to earn better than a 'C,' the idea must be feasible." So said a professor at Yale University on a paper turned in by one **Fred Smith**. The paper envisioned a company that provided reliable overnight delivery; Smith went on to found Federal Express.

A CONFEDERACY OF DUNCES: THE ARTS & LITERATURE EDITION

In 1917, **F. Scott Fitzgerald** dropped out of Princeton to enlist in World War I. Already committed to becoming a writer, Fitzgerald worried he'd die in battle and the world would never know about his talent, so during his military training stateside, he dashed off a novel called *The Romantic Egotist*. It was well-received, although ultimately rejected, by an editor at Scribner's. As it happened, the war ended before Fitzgerald could be sent to Europe—allowing him to write such classics as *The Great Gatsby* before he had a heart attack, probably exacerbated by alcoholism, in the midst of writing what might have been his greatest novel, *The Love of the Last Tycoon*, in 1940.

After submitting his magnum opus *Remembrance of Things Past* to an important publisher, **Marcel Proust** received the following response from an editor: "I may be dead from the neck up, but rack my brains as I may I can't see why a chap should need thirty pages to describe how he turns over in bed before going to sleep." English lit majors everywhere have been asking themselves that same question ever since Proust *did* get his entire masterwork published, at his own expense, in 1927.

Vincent van Gogh famously never sold a painting during his lifetime, but all the dunces weren't quite in confederacy against him. For one thing, he'd only been painting for a decade when he committed suicide, and for another thing, he began receiving high praise for his works in the months before he died. In fact, some have argued that Van Gogh found the accolades more disturbing than he had the failure.

The record label **Decca** has the distinction of making the worst blunder in all of popular music. In 1962, a Decca memo read, "We don't like their sound. Groups of guitars are on the way out." The "they" in question was the Beatles, and as it happened, guitar music was *not* on the way out. **Columbia Records** also rejected the Beatles—at which point John Lennon must have started thinking his Aunt Mimi had been right. "The guitar's all right for a hobby," he once quoted her as saying, "but it won't earn you any money."

Collecting Rejections

Garnering rejections is a badge of honor in some corners of the publishing world, but few will match the purple hearts won by these brave souls:

- Richard Bach's *Jonathan Livingston Seagull* was rejected by 26 publishers.
- Richard Hooker's *M*A*S*H* was turned down 21 times.
- James Joyce's modernist classic *Dubliners* was rejected by 22 publishers.
- Dr. Seuss' *To Think That I Saw It on Mulberry Street* was rejected by 27 publishers.
- Between magazine pitches, short stories, and books, Jack London claimed to have received 600 rejections.

By the early 1930s, **e. e. cummings** had established his literary credibility with a novelized memoir called *The Enormous Room* and several books of experimental poetry. Having finished 71 new poems, he decided to submit them for publication. The book was rejected by 14 different publishers. Finally, in

- British mystery novelist John Creasey (1908–1973) garnered a staggering 743 rejection slips—all for books! What's more remarkable is that Creasey went on to write and publish at least 562 novels (he lost count) in his 40-year career, making him one of the most prolific novelists in history.

1935, cummings's mom subsidized the book's publication. He called it *No Thanks*, and where the title page would have been, he wrote *TO* and then the names of every publisher who'd rejected him, typed out in the shape of an urn.

When **John Kennedy Toole** (1937–1969) finished his first novel, *A Confederacy of Dunces*, he was convinced it was a comic masterpiece. He sent it away to Simon & Schuster, who eventually rejected the book on the grounds that it "isn't really about anything." Toole became despondent after that single rejection (if only he'd seen the sidebar above) and ended up committing suicide. But the novel was eventually published thanks to his mom, who got the writer Walker Percy to read *Dunces*. Percy loved it—and 22 years after Toole's death, his masterpiece won the Pulitzer Prize.

PATRON GENIUSES

There's a patron saint for everything. Really. Got hemmorhoids? Ask for the intercession of St. Fiacre. Praying for a new HD-ready TV? Won't hurt to ask the assistance of St. Clare of Assisi, who is the patron saint of television (mainly because when she was too ill to attend church, an image of the mass would appear on her wall like a heavenly flat screen). But if patron saints aren't doing the trick, you can always turn to Patron Geniuses.

Patron Geniuses of Incarcerated Criminals:

Bill Gates. That's right: If you're facing 20 to life at Riker's and need a genius shoulder on which to cry, turn to the mega-billionaire founder of Microsoft, because he knows the troubles you've seen. Although he admittedly lacks the homemade tattoos, Bill Gates really did spend some time in the clink. Contrary to popular belief, Gates was always wealthy—his father was a prominent lawyer in Seattle—and so by the time Gates was 22, he already owned a Porsche 911. Not so nerdy after all! Police caught Gates racing the Porsche in New Mexico on December 13, 1977, and he spent part of that day (although not the night) in an Albuquerque jail.

Patron Genius of Perfectionists:

Johannes Brahms was a perfectionist in most facets of his life—although he was not such a perfectionist when it came to beard maintenance. But when it came to music, he felt compelled to get it right, which led to four brilliant symphonies and two piano concertos, among other pieces. But his perfectionism had a down side: It's believed that Brahms actually composed more than four symphonies, but destroyed the ones he felt didn't live up to his reputation, a decision the world has long lamented.

Patron Genius Against Constipation:

Martin Luther suffered from severe constipation throughout his life, and perhaps as a result, his writings are filled with scatological references, particularly when referencing the Devil. ("I scared him away with my flatulence," Luther once wrote of the Man Downstairs.) Some have even speculated that Luther's suffering led him to his more self-flagellating ascetic life, which in turn pushed him away from the then-decadent Catholic Church and toward nailing those 95 theses on the door of Wittenberg's Church of All Saints.

Patron Genius of Obsessives:

Think you're obsessed with your ex-boyfriend just because you google him daily and weep for him every night? That's child's play compared to **Dante Alighieri,** the Italian poet and author of *The Divine Comedy*, who held a candle for his beloved Beatrice for almost 50 years—even though he only met her twice. They first became acquainted when Dante was 9 and Beatrice was 8.

Of seeing her that first time, Dante later wrote, "Behold, a deity stronger than I; who coming, shall rule over me." They met once more, nine years later, on the street in Florence, for about ten seconds. From that little interaction, Dante managed to write a whole book of poems for Beatrice, called *La Vita Nuova (New Life)*. Dante acted upset that Beatrice married a banker in 1287—but you rarely hear that he himself had married two years earlier. He never, incidentally, wrote a book of love poems about his wife.

Patron Geniuses of Syphilis

As much as they get the TB, they also tend toward the VD. It's true, geniuses are drawn to syphilis like flies to honey, so be careful out there, friends. Just some of the Patron Geniuses Against Syphilis you might want to keep on hand: Vincent van Gogh, Toulouse Latrec, Oscar Wilde, Paul Gauguin, Leo Tolstoy, Gustav Flaubert, Franz Schubert, Howard Hughes, and Friedrich Nietzsche.

GENIUSES AND PANCAKES

As we shall see, the budding genius has much to learn from the pancake:

The Pancake Sorting Problem:

Imagine that you have a stack of circular pancakes, wherein—because you are apparently a very bad pancake maker—each pancake has a different diameter. The pancakes are stacked randomly, and your job, using a spatula, is to stack them in order of size, with the biggest on the bottom. You may enter the spatula at any point in the stack, and then flip what's on top of your spatula over. Because the imaginary pancakes are getting cold and we're hungry, you'll need to accomplish this task in as few flips as possible.

Sound interesting? Probably not, but the Pancake Sorting Problem has fascinated people for decades, mostly because of its implications for certain computer networks. In fact, the only technical paper Bill Gates ever wrote, alluringly titled "Bounds for Sorting by Prefix Reversal" and published in that scintillating gossip rag known as *Discrete Mathematics* in 1979, was devoted to an algorithm for a more efficient pancake-sorting system than had ever been discovered before!

The Lazy Caterer's Sequence

The Lazy Caterer's Sequence is a sequence of numbers that tells the maximum number of pieces one can get from making a minimal number of cuts to a pancake. That is, one cut can give you two pieces, two cuts four pieces, three cuts seven pieces (not of equal size), four cuts eleven pieces, and so on. The sequence is relevant to some abstract mathematics problems but, mostly, mathematicians just like finding weird number sequences. Of course, none of this explains the real questions at the center of the lazy caterer's sequence, which are: Why would a lazy caterer cut up pancakes instead of just making smaller pancakes? And furthermore, would a genuinely *lazy* caterer even serve pancakes in the first place? Wouldn't she or he rather serve, like, microwaved beans and weenies?

Pancake Flatness

So how flat is a pancake? Hillier, it turns out, than Kansas. In 2003, a group of scientists from Southwest Texas State University and Arizona State University (apparently, such meaningful scientific investigations require two university science programs) analyzed the topography of both the state of Kansas and a pancake they bought at IHOP. Their conclusion? "Simply put, our results show that Kansas is considerably flatter than a pancake." The researchers acknowledged that "barring the acquisition of a Kansas-sized pancake or a pancake-sized Kansas," it was difficult to truly compare the two, but the terrain of a pancake, when magnified tens of thousands of times anyway, is actually quite rugged.

Regardless, Kansas *isn't* the flattest state. Measuring by the difference between highest and lowest elevations, Kansas is actually 22nd. Florida is the flattest state. As one Kansan said in response to the study, "I think this is part of a vast breakfast food conspiracy to denigrate Kansas." We're just wondering where we can get a Kansas-sized pancake. (For the record: The world's largest pancake was cooked in Rochdale, England in 1994; it weighed more than three tons.)

YOUR MODEL MATH GENIUS: GEORG CANTOR

When it comes to abstract mathematics, even when math is about numbers, it's not *really* about numbers—which should come as a relief to all you budding geniuses who still have nightmares about finding the area of a circle given only the circumference. So in the spirit of numberless math, we are now going to introduce you to German mathematician Georg "Hold the E" Cantor, who was arguably the most important mathematician of the 19th century, *without using a single number*. Well, except the 19th in the preceding sentence. And then that second 19th. And there's another 19th. Oh, man, we're getting ourselves into an infinite set, which Cantor, as it happened, studied.

As long as you're talking about apples and oranges and Bobby Brown fans, there's no need for infinite sets, because they're always countable. But when you start thinking about numbers as abstractions, things get a little kooky. There are many, many infinite sets of numbers. An infinite number of them, actually. The set of all integers is infinite, for instance, and so is the set of all non-integers. And although we often view the infinity symbol— ∞ —as a number meaning "a lot," ∞ isn't a really big number: Not to get all metaphysical on you or anything, but ∞ is an expression of boundlessness. As such, it doesn't behave in the normal, nice way a number does. The weirdness of infinities was first pointed out by the Greek philosopher Zeno in his famous Achilles Paradox, which goes like this:

Achilles and a tortoise decide they're going to have a footrace. But because Achilles is fast, he gives the tortoise a head start. Then Achilles takes off. Before Achilles can pass the tortoise, he has to make up the initial gap. And in the time that takes him, the tortoise will move a little farther. And then Achilles will have to make up *that* gap, during which time the tortoise will move a bit farther—so theoretically, Achilles can never pass the tortoise.

Now, the easy solution to this paradox is just to shut up and let Achilles run past the tortoise before you get a headache trying to figure out the mathematics of why passing the tortoise is supposedly impossible, which is pretty much what everyone did for millennia. That is, until Georg Cantor showed up. From the beginning of his career, Cantor was as fascinated by the philosophical implications of math as he was by math itself. While mathematics dissertation titles usually look like fractions giving birth to a random string of Greek letters, the title of Cantor's dissertation was "In Mathematics the Art of Asking Questions is More Valuable Than Solving Problems."

Cantor's questions about numbers eventually led to his mind-boggling solution to Zeno's Achilles Paradox, which we won't get into here, because A) it's boring, and B) we don't really understand it. But one of Cantor's central proofs showed that some infinities are bigger than other infinities (like the tiny infinity the tortoise has just moved). Thus, Cantor claimed, the infinite set of real numbers can be proven bigger than the infinite set of rational numbers. In fact, Cantor's Theorem also implies the existence of a sort of overarching infinity known as the "infinity of infinities." Cantor, whose bipolar disorder worsened as he aged, thought this proved his personal God-as-numbers theory, but while that's a bit of a stretch, some mathematicians do have an almost mystical appreciation for Cantor. As fellow mathematician David Hilbert put it, "No one shall expel us from the Paradise that Cantor has created for us."

Not a Model Literary Genius

The one thing about Cantor that most aspiring math geniuses would like to avoid is his mental illness, which led him to spend his last years in a sanitarium. Among his more eccentric hobbies was trying to prove that scientist and essayist Sir Francis Bacon was the secret author of William Shakespeare's plays.

SOME THINGS TO KNOW ABOUT THE AWARDS YOU'RE SOON TO WIN

Nobel

Cash Money: More than $1.3 million in 2006.

Number Given Annually: Six (Physics, Chemistry, Medicine, Literature, Economics, and Peace)

Who It's Named For: Alfred Nobel, the Swedish chemist who invented dynamite. Nobel may have decided to fund the prizes after a premature obituary of him was published by a French newspaper under the headline "The Merchant of Death Is Dead." Nobel, a pacifist who designed dynamite to be a safer explosive, was horrified to think that he might be remembered only as a killer. So he used the bulk of his estate to endow the prizes, which almost immediately became *the* international award most craved by geniuses.

Anecdotally: A longstanding but probably untrue rumor claims that Nobel refused to create a prize in mathematics because a girl he was once engaged to cheated on him with a mathematician.

Fields Medal

Cash Money: $15,000 Canadian

Number Given: Between two and four, once every four years. Like the Olympics. Only for math.

Who It's Named For: John Charles Fields (1863–1932), a Canadian professor of mathematics who in 1924 happened to be president of the Royal Canadian Institute. The International Congress of Mathematics that year had a surplus of cash after printing the programs, so they decided to award prizes to two outstanding young mathematicians. Fields left part of his estate to endow the prize at each International Congress, and included in his will the unambiguous statement that the award should *not* be named after him. His silly Canadian modesty was promptly ignored.

Anecdotally: Only mathematicians under 40 are eligible for the Fields Medal, so if you're

The Ig Nobels

Cash Money: $0
Number Given Annually: Varies
Who It's Named For: Nobody. The Ig Nobels are awarded each year for achievements that "first make people laugh, and then make them think." Past winners include professors who taught pigeons to distinguish between the work of Picasso and Monet; the authors of the "deeply penetrating" scholarly article "Rectal Foreign Bodies: Case Reports and a Comprehensive Review of the World's Literature;" a physicist whose work explains why shower curtains billow inward; a scientist's comprehensive survey of human belly button lint; and a 2002 study by three Swedish professors entitled "Chickens Prefer Beautiful Humans." And not just chickens: An Ig Nobel was also awarded to a

researcher who established that the presence of humans tends to sexually arouse ostriches. *Anecdotally:* During the annual presentation of the Ig Nobels, the crowd traditionally throws a variety of complex paper airplanes onto the stage (you've gotta learn to love this geek stuff if you want to be a genius!). Harvard physics professor Roy Glauber is traditionally the "Keeper of the Broom;" i.e., the guy who sweeps up the paper airplanes. But in 2005, he had to take the year off. Why? Because he was needed in Stockholm to collect a real Nobel.

over the hill, forget math and take up writing musicals or something.

Tony

Cash Money: $0

Number Given Annually: 29 in 2006

Who It's Named For: Mary Antoinette Perry, whose name inspires a question in and of itself: If you're going to *almost* name your daughter after a famously snobby decapitated French monarch, why not just go the extra mile and make that Mary a Marie? Regardless, Perry made her New York acting debut in 1905 and became one of Broadway's most successful actresses and directors. Shortly after her death in 1946, the American Theater Wing, which she'd helped found, established the Antoinette Perry Award for Excellence in Theatre in her honor.

Anecdotally: Only plays produced at Broadway theaters are eligible for Tony Awards. Curiously enough, of the 39 current Broadway theater houses, only six sport addresses actually on Broadway in New York. Most are located just *off* Broadway, which only further confuses matters, because some "off-Broadway" theaters have addresses *on* Broadway. Here's the difference:

Broadway theaters generally have more than 500 seats, off-Broadway theaters between 100 and 499, and off-off-Broadway have fewer than 100.

The Man Booker Award

Cash Money: £50,000 (about $87,500)

Number Given Annually: One for the original award, although there's now a Man Booker International Prize and a Man Booker Russian Prize

Who It's Named For: When first awarded in 1969, it was originally known as the "Booker-McConnell" prize, Booker-McConnell being the frozen food wholesaling company that sponsored the prize. When that company was bought out by a frozen food company in Iceland (because, hey, it's an easy place to freeze stuff), a stockbrokerage named the Man Group took over sponsorship. Awarded annually to one full-length novel written by an author from the UK, the British Commonwealth, or Ireland, the Booker has long been one of the world's premier literary awards.

Anecdotally: The most nominated novelist in history was Iris Murdoch (whose struggle with Alzheimer's was dramatized in the Oscar-winning *Iris*). Murdoch made it to the Booker Prize shortlist six times, but won only once—for *The Sea, The Sea* in 1978.

Oscar

Cash Money: $0

Number Given Annually: 24, not counting the scientific and technical awards.

Who It's Named For: That's a very good question. First awarded in 1928, the Academy Awards were known as the Oscars within a decade, but no one knows for sure just how it happened. There are three competing theories:

1. Bette Davis claimed she named the statuette "Oscar" because its butt resembled that of her first husband, Oscar Nelson.

2. Newspaper columnist Sidney Skolsky argued he started calling the awards the Oscars in order to keep them from becoming a pretentious affair. (Um, Mission Not Accomplished.)

3. Margaret Herrick (1902–1976), the librarian of the Academy of Motion Pictures Arts and Sciences for more than 40 years, is often credited with the name. When she first saw the statuettes, Herrick reportedly said, "They look just like my Uncle Oscar."

Anecdotally: Directors who've never won an Academy Award include Alfred Hitchcock, Stanley Kubrick, Ingmar Bergman, and Federico Fellini.

The Pulitzers

Cash Money: $10,000, except for the winner in the Public Service category, who gets not one thin dime.

Number Given Annually: 21, from Beat Reporting to Poetry to Music

Who It's Named For: Joseph Pulitzer, the newspaper publisher who made TV news talk shows possible by introducing America to sensationalized, unfair, and avowedly unbalanced reporting. Born in Hungary, Pulitzer came to America in 1864 to fight in the Civil War. After the war, he moved to St. Louis and bought the *St. Louis Dispatch* for $2,700. Pulitzer was an unscrupulous businessman with a bad reputation; Columbia University initially turned down his offer to fund a journalism school there because they didn't want to be associated with his name. But eventually Columbia relented and took his money. They also administer the prize his estate established in his name.

Anecdotally: Let's get our pronunciation right, once and for all. According to the Pulitzer Prize's Web site, the correct pronunciation is "PULL-it-sir," not "PEW-litz-er."

30%

genius

You're certainly getting there. According to our calculations, your current level of genius is approximately equal to that of Chicago artist Eduardo Kac, who in 2000 convinced a French laboratory to make him a glowing bunny rabbit. (You'll note that you are not quite enough of a genius to make your *own* glowing bunny.) By injecting GFP (green fluorescent protein) plucked from a jellyfish into a fertilized rabbit egg. The resulting creature, whom Kac called Alba, looks like a normal albino rabbit—except under black light, its fur, eyes, and whiskers glow a *Simpsons*-style uranium green. In short, you're not quite ready to make breakthroughs that save, or even improve, civilization. In fact, at this point, most of your major creations will likely make the world a slightly worse place (at least for bunnies). But don't fret! You're well on your way: Today, glow-in-the-dark bunnies. Tomorrow, the world!

TIME TRAVEL

Einstein's theory of relativity, which you incidentally might want to freshen up on (see p. 16), had all kinds of crazy implications. For instance, general relativity proved that, because space-time is curved, lines that start out parallel can cross (no matter what your 10th grade geometry teacher taught you).

And special relativity proved that time is not absolute. Some argue that the combination of space-time curvature and the relativity of time means that it might really be possible to build a time machine that can travel into the past. As part of physicists' broad attempt to make their studies absolutely impenetrable to normal people, past-traveling time machines employ, in the jargon of physics, a "closed, timelike curve."

But first, let's deal with time machines that take you into the future. Good news! They already exist. They're called airplanes. Einstein's theory of special relativity dictates that the experience of time is relative to motion. Basically, the faster you travel, the slower you age.

Imagine that you have two ex-girlfriends, Julie and Karen, who happen to have been born at the exact same moment on the exact same day. Thanks to your ceaseless Internet stalking, you've found out that Julie has become a successful romance novelist, while Karen pilots commercial jets. With your comprehensive understanding of special relativity, you know that, despite their identical birth moments, Julie the novelist is now older than Karen the pilot—because those who travel at high speeds age more slowly. That is, it takes them less time to get to the future than it takes us.

Admittedly, the difference an airplane makes is pretty miniscule: If Julie has traveled 550,000 miles in an airplane, she has traveled approximately 1 microsecond into the future. But when you approach the speed of light, the difference can become dramatic—so, theoretically, a very fast-moving airplane could send you markedly (well, a couple seconds) into the future.

A Couple of Complications

The problem is that once you get into the future, there may be no way for you to return to the past. No less a genius than physicist Stephen Hawking has hypothesized that the laws of physics cannot allow for backward time travel—partly because of the philosophical paradoxes it would involve (see sidebar). The easiest way to travel into the past would be to exceed the speed of light—at least relative to the earth, since faster-than-light travel would be seen as occurring backward through time. Unfortunately for science fiction TV shows everywhere, exceeding the speed of light is probably impossible.

But there are other ways. In 1948, Einstein's walking buddy and fellow New Jerseyan-by-way-of-Europe, Kurt Gödel, proposed that the universe may be rotating. If this were true, the spinning of the universe would also result in the spinning of light. Godel hypothesized that this might make it possible to enter a closed time loop, allowing you to travel back in time *without* exceeding the speed of light.

Such wormholes provide the most exciting possibilities for backward time travel, which is why pretty much 100 percent of the programming on the Sci Fi Channel is devoted to them. As previously noted, we know from general relativity that gravity warps space-time. This means that, theoretically, a curve might be so deep that it connects two points in space:

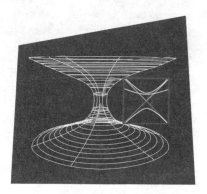

Wormholes amount to shortcuts through the universe. But in order to function as time machines to the past, a number of conditions would need to be met:

1. Wormholes would have to actually exist. No one knows for sure whether they do, although many physicists believe they are certainly possible.

2. Wormholes would have to be stabilized somehow. To stop the wormhole from imploding and just turning into a black hole, something in or near the wormhole would need to produce a lot of the negative pressure force known as anti-gravity.

The Philosophy of Time Travel

Philosophers have long been fascinated with the implications of backward time travel, because philosophers love paradoxes and questions of causality, and time travel has plenty of both. Take these two:

1. Suppose you go into the future and read a book. Say, this book. Then you go back to the past, and then you call us up and say, "You guys should write a book about becoming a genius. Put something in it about time travel." We then write the book. But who came up with the idea? Not us, because you told us about it. And not you, because you read about it in the future. The book *had* to exist in the future, and yet it—seemingly—could not have existed without you traveling into the future. Anyway, that's a weird paradox, but thanks for the idea about the book!

2. The classic time travel paradox: If you travel into the past, and you kill your mother while she is just a child, wouldn't you, then, never have existed? And wouldn't your mother, therefore, not have been killed by you? For a thoughtful meditation on this paradox, check out the work of Immanuel Kant, or *Back to the Future Part II*.

3. One mouth of the wormhole would need to be towed (Note: This would require one heck of a tugboat) close to the surface of a neutron star (which is a kind of collapsed supernova in which the force of gravity is so strong that it slows time). So that,

4. The two sides of the wormhole would accumulate a time difference, allowing you to jump into the past,

with the one caveat being that you can't travel into a time before your wormhole time machine was created.

So is it theoretically possible? Maybe. But don't start fantasizing about dinosaur huntin' just yet.

IF IT'S TOO LATE FOR YOU: THE SCIENCE EDITION

Looking to raise a scientific genius? Fitting your wee ones with an adorable little lab coat will help, but you might also try some of these proven strategies:

Strategy 1: Let them tinker

Worked for: **Richard Feynman** (1918–1988), one of the 20th century's greatest physicists. Feynman's IQ was measured at 124 when he was young—well above average, but far from genius level. So how'd he become fluent in differential equations by the age of 15? Feynman's fascination with the inner workings of the mechanical objects around him couldn't have hurt his left-brain power. As a kid living in Queens, he took apart everything from radios to wagon wheels. This wide-eyed fascination stuck with him; for his entire life, Feynman's colleagues cited his "childlike" approach to physics problems, which bore great results. In fact, a fellow physicist once said that the "Feynman Problem Solving Algorithm" contained three steps: 1. Write down the problem. 2. Think very hard. 3. Write down the answer.

Strategy 2: Abandon your children and then return years later in a vain attempt to turn them into farmers

Worked for: **Isaac Newton** (1643–1727). Newton was born three months after his father's death, and by the time he was 2, his mother had abandoned Isaac to run off and marry a minister, for whom Isaac harbored an intense hatred throughout his childhood. So Isaac was raised by his grandmother, who saw to it that he attended school. An extraordinarily bright student, Newton had a promising future. But then the minister died, and Isaac's mother returned to his life, and this time nearly succeeded in ruining it: She insisted that Isaac farm her land. Teenage Isaac, needless to say, made a pretty poor vegetable farmer. She eventually allowed Newton to go back to school, making possible the discovery of three laws of motion, calculus, classic mechanics, and—if you believe the stories—the cat flap.

Strategy 3: Make sure your kids hang out with nerds

Worked for: **Linus Pauling** (1901–1994). The only person ever to win two unshared Nobel Prizes, chemist Linus Pauling was a smart kid. When he was 9, Pauling's father sent a letter to the editor of the local paper asking which books he should buy his son, adding, "And don't say the Bible or Darwin's *Origin of Species*, because he already read them." But what led Pauling toward chemistry was a visit to his nerdy friend Lloyd Jeffress's house when Pauling was 13. Lloyd had just gotten a chemistry set and showed Linus how you can get steaming black carbon when you mix sugar and sulfuric acid (man, they don't make chemistry sets like they used to). Linus went on to become the greatest chemist of the century, despite dropping out of high school. And Lloyd Jeffress? He and Pauling remained close friends for life.

Strategy 4: Let everyone think your kid is slow, even though he's obviously not

Worked for: **Albert Einstein** (1879–1955). Although he is remembered as a poor student whose innate genius went undeveloped until his 20s, Einstein was in fact very bright from the start. He may have suffered from dyslexia, which could have confused his teachers—but he was never *that* bad of a student. Einstein was reading the impenetrable philosophy of Immanuel Kant when he was just 10, taught himself Euclidian geometry when he was 12, and was only 16 when—while staring in the mirror—he imagined what would happen to his face if he were to travel at the speed of light. As far as we're concerned, you're pretty smart if, at 16, you look into the mirror, and instead of combing your rather unruly hair, you come to the revolutionary conclusion that the speed of light is constant regardless of the observer's speed.

IF IT'S TOO LATE
FOR YOU: THE ART &
LITERATURE EDITION

Strategy 1: Start 'em young

Worked for: **Pablo Picasso** (1881–1973). You know that Picasso was the son of a painter because only an *artiste* would name his son Pablo Diego José Santiago Francisco de Paula Juan Nepomuceno Crispín Crispiniano de los Remedios Cipriano de la Santísima Trinidad Ruiz Picasso. We know Spanish names are often long, but that's just crazy. Correct us if we're wrong, but do we see *both* a Crispín *and* a Crispiniano in there? Wouldn't one or the other have sufficed? At any rate, when Pablo was little, he often watched his father paint. His first word, in fact, was *piz*, a shortening of the Spanish *lapiz*, or pencil. Pablo landed his first exhibition at 13, by which time the boy's success had become his dad's primary goal in life—in short, Picasso was the Macaulay Culkin of his time.

Strategy 2: Be a pretty normal upper-middle-class family, so your kid will rebel against that bourgeois world and grow a fascinatingly weird mustache

Worked for: **Salvador Dalí** (1904–1989). The son of a Spanish lawyer, Salvador Dalí was blessed with two parents who supported his artwork from the very beginning—when Dalí was 13, his dad even put together an exhibition of Dalí's work in the family home. Although they had their tragedies—Dalí had an older brother who died before he was born and whose shoes he always felt he needed to fill—the Dalí family was pretty white-bread. But when Dalí was 16, his mother died, and then his dad ended up marrying his dead mom's sister—a fact that Dalí resented. And while that may have sparked the budding surrealist's increasingly eccentric behavior and dress, at least some of it was just good old-fashioned rebellion.

Strategy 3: Absolutely refuse to allow them to become artists

Worked for: **Michelangelo** (1475–1564). The great Renaissance artist and sculptor grew up in a moderately wealthy family in Florence. His father owned a marble quarry—Michelangelo later noted that he "sucked in chisels and hammers with my mother's milk"—but that didn't mean that Dad liked artists. Quite the opposite. When Michelangelo was a child, his father would literally beat him for refusing to pick a nobler profession. But all the beatings came to naught: When he was just 13, Michelangelo began an apprenticeship with a painter and quickly established himself as a formidable young talent.

Strategy 4: Dress your boys in girls' clothing

Worked for: Both **Ernest Hemingway** (1899–1961) and **Oscar Wilde** (1854–1900), amazingly enough. Lady Jane Wilde was an eccentric poet and advocate for women's rights who desperately wanted a daughter. What she got instead, an Oscar, was a good enough mannequin for her: Most scholars argue that the young Oscar exclusively wore girls' clothes in his toddler years. But before you try to connect Oscar's gender-bending upbringing to his homosexuality, bear in mind that no less a macho hunk than Ernest Hemingway was similarly raised—and apparently for the same reason. Hemingway's mom, in fact, dressed Ernest in girls' clothes into his teenage years—and generally tried to make him an identical twin to his older sister, Marcelline.

CORRESPOND LIKE A GENIUS

One thing to remember about becoming a genius: You can now depend on the fact that much of your correspondence will be preserved in a university library and eventually be made into a multi-volume reference work, edited by a professor whose entire career is devoted to the study and appreciation of you. So to help you stop forwarding "yo mama" jokes and start writing the kind of correspondence expected of a genius, we've collected some handy tips.

Tip 1: BREVITY IS THE SOUL OF WIT

Remember, now that you're a genius, you're not just writing to one person. You're also writing to all the people who will later read your correspondence to glean insight into your genius. Keep your audience interested by keeping your thoughts short and punchy. Dorothy Parker, for instance, once wrote a cable to a friend who'd just had a baby: "Good work, Mary. We all knew you had it in you." And in 1965, Groucho Marx famously wrote to a Hollywood club: "Please accept my resignation. I don't care to belong to any club that will have me as a member."

Tip 2: A LITTLE LITERARY FLAIR WILL GO A LONG WAY

For proof of this, we need look no further than the great Southern novelist William Faulkner, who was obviously tired of his job at the post office in Oxford, Mississippi, when he penned the following letter to the Postmaster General: "As long as I live under the capitalist system," Faulkner wrote, "I expect to have my life influenced by the demands of moneyed people. But I will be damned if I propose to be at the beck and call of every itinerant scoundrel who has two cents to invest in a postage stamp. This, sir, is my resignation."

Tip 3: DON'T BE AFRAID TO SHOW A LITTLE SASS

Although we often look at past presidents as a genteel, well-mannered lot, they could be plenty sassy. When an admirer asked Abraham Lincoln for a "sentiment" and an autograph, for instance, Lincoln wrote back: "Dear Madam, when you ask from a stranger that which is of interest only to yourself, always enclose a stamp. There's your sentiment, and here's your autograph. *Abraham Lincoln*." A century later, Harry "My Entire Middle Name Was S" Truman showed less humor but more vitriol when writing to a newspaperman who'd just unfavorably reviewed a concert by Truman's daughter: "Some day I hope to meet you," Truman wrote to the reporter. "When that happens, you'll need a new nose, a lot of beefsteak for black eyes, and perhaps a supporter below!"

Tip 4: BUT IF YOU HAVE SOMETHING REALLY MEAN TO SAY, HAVE SOMEONE ELSE SAY IT

Writers Mark Twain and William Dean Howells were great friends, and at the top of their profession, when Mark Twain wrote the following letter:

To the editor,

Sir to you, I would like to know what kind of a goddam govment this is that discriminates between two economic carriers & makes a goddam railroad charge everybody equal & lets a goddam man charge any goddam price he wants to for his goddam opera box.

—W. D. Howells

Howells, it is an outrage the way the govment is acting so I sent this complaint to the N. Y. Times with your name signed because it would have more weight. Mark

Tip 5: TRY TO CORRESPOND WITH OTHER GENIUSES

This offers an excellent opportunity to really display your wit and intelligence against the world's finest minds. For example, when playwright George Bernard Shaw invited Winston Churchill to the opening night of Shaw's newest play, he wrote, "Have reserved two tickets for my first night. Come and bring a friend, if you have one." Churchill replied, "Impossible to come first night. Will come second night, if you have one."

Tip 6: IF YOU, PERCHANCE, INVENT A NEW METHOD OF CORRESPONDENCE, SAY SOMETHING MEMORABLE

Samuel Morse did all right when he sent the world's first telegraph: "What hath God wrought?" That will suffice; just don't end up like computer engineer Ray Tomlinson. When Tomlinson sent the world's first e-mail in 1971, he failed so miserably at making it memorable that even he himself does not exactly remember what he wrote. Tomlinson's best guess? "Qwertyuiop."

PEACE: TREATIES EVERY POLITICAL GENIUS NEEDS TO KNOW

Versailles

The fighting part of World War I ended, of course, on the eleventh hour of the eleventh month of the eleventh day of the eleventh year (well, the eleventh year after 1907). But it took six months before the actual peace treaty—known as the Treaty of Versailles—was signed by all parties. For a document that took so long to draft, it sure didn't work very well. The treaty held Germany entirely responsible for all "loss and damage" suffered by the Allied countries, which meant Germany owed France a lot of money. Some have blamed the excessive reparations required of Germany for the collapse of the Weimar Republic and the rise of Nazism. On the upside, the Treaty of Versailles did create an independent Poland for the first time in two centuries, a nation that lasted almost 21 years before Germany and Russia—who, historically, just cannot help themselves when it comes to Poland invading—carved it up again.

Nuclear Non-Proliferation Treaty

First signed by military powerhouse Finland in 1968, the Nuclear Non-Proliferation Treaty (or NPT to those in the know) now counts 188 sovereign states as signatories. Like a dog with a funny gait, the treaty has three legs:

1. **Non-proliferation.** Only five nations are allowed to have nuclear weapons: China, the U.S., Russia, the UK, and France. All other countries agree not to develop nuclear weapons. These five nations agree not to give nuclear technology to anyone else, and they agree not to hit non-nuclear nations with nuclear weapons.
   Successfulness: Eh. India, Pakistan, North Korea, and Israel also have nuclear weapons, a fact that the present incarnation of the NPT just sort of ignores.

2. **Disarmament:** This part of the treaty says that nuclear states should attempt to reduce and eventually eliminate their weapons stockpiles.
   Successfulness: Total failure.

3. **The right to peacefully use nuclear technology:** Non-nuclear states are allowed to use nuclear power, but if they start to use it for weapons, they are in big trouble.
   Successfulness: This part has actually worked pretty well.
   All in all, the treaty has a spotty record when it comes to countries adhering to it. But it's certainly fared a heck of a lot better than:

Treaties of Paris: A Timeline

It's the city of lights, the city of mimes and great wines and quick surrender. But above all, it's the city of treaties:

1259: England agrees to stop invading France. Tragically, England finds the temptation too strong, and just 70 years later starts invading France like crazy, beginning a 116-year conflict known as the Hundred Years' War.

1763: Britain, France, and Spain agree to end the Seven Years' War.

1783: The Treaty of Paris formally ends the American Revolution. After the treaty's ratification, John Jay, John Adams, and Ben Franklin get drunk at a restaurant that still exists and is now *also* known as the Treaty of Paris.

1814: The Napoleonic Wars come to an end—well, more of a break than an end, really.

The Bajillion American Indian Treaties

The United States government broke dozens of treaties with American Indian tribes, and each was horrible in its own special way. From the Treaty of Buffalo Creek in present-day New York to the Treaty of Chicago, all Indian treaties had the same central theme: We, the U.S. government, hereby offer you a small amount of money, which incidentally there's about a 30 percent chance we'll pay, in exchange for a few million acres of land. You, the American Indians, agree to move west. After a while, we will make our way west as well, whereupon we will offer you a small amount of money in exchange for a few million acres of land, until finally you live primarily in Oklahoma and South Dakota which, honestly, you can have for all we care. You further agree to allow, in the distant future, one of the Village People to dress in an extraordinarily offensive approximation of your sacred attire; in exchange, we give you the right to open casinos so you might slowly but surely take your money back from us.

1815: Following Napoleon's defeat at Waterloo, the Napoleonic Wars *really* come to an end.

1898: The Spanish–American War ends. Good news for America, and better news for Teddy Roosevelt, who gets to abandon a life of suicidal charges up hills for the simple pleasures of elected office.

1973: The Paris Peace Accords, presumably so called because "The Treaty of Paris" was starting to sound cliché, ends American involvement in the Vietnam War.

40%

genius

Congratulations! You are now 40% of the way toward full-fledged Genius.

This is a very dangerous level of geniusity, so you will need to push through the next several pages to come out on the other side. Right now, you're at what we in the field of geniology (the study of genius, and also the study of genies) like to call the "know-it-all-but-doesn't" stage. At this point, you may find yourself overwhelmed by the urge to correct every error and misconception you come across. That's all fine and well— geniuses should be at least a *tad* annoying. But you don't want to suffer the indignity, for instance, of telling an English professor who's rambling on about "Don JEW-on," that Byron's epic poem *Don Juan* should be pronounced "don WAN." Because in that case, you'd be wrong. (We know Byron called his central character "Don JEW-on" because otherwise, much of the meter and rhyme scheme wouldn't make sense.)

GREEKING HAVOC: IMPORTANT GREEKS WHO CHANGED EVERYTHING

First, we'll tackle the philosophical biggies:

Socrates (470–399 BCE)

Invented the Socratic method, wherein you ask someone a series of questions in an attempt either to get at some philosophical truth, or else to annoy people to such a degree that eventually you're forced to commit suicide by eating hemlock. We know about Socrates mostly because of his early pupil

Plato (427–347 BCE),

whose *Dialogues* remain required reading in philosophy classes. Plato was among the first writers to confront questions of nature versus nurture, ideal government, and the nature of knowledge. One of his students,

Aristotle (384–322 BCE),

is often considered the first empiricist, because he chiefly valued knowledge gleaned from the five senses. For a guy who is thought of as a founding father of modern philosophical inquiry, though,

Aristotle was wrong a staggering percentage of the time. Like, for a guy who ostensibly gained knowledge via his senses, he could have used either touch or sight to realize he was dead wrong in believing that men had more teeth than women.

Sophocles (c. 495–406 BCE)

Along with Euripides and Aeschylus, Sophocles was one of the great tragic playwrights in ancient Greece. Most well-known for his plays about Oedipus and Antigone, Sophocles was also a general in the Greek army, a priest, and—in his younger days—one of the star members of a boy band who only performed naked. (Seriously.) But he was most famous for his dramatic work: Aristotle called Sophocles's *Oedipus Rex* the perfect tragedy.

Pythagoras (c. 582–507 BCE)

Scholars agree that the Greek philosopher, mathematician, and cult leader did *not* come up with the Pythagorean theorem. Pythagoras started a brotherhood (No Girls Allowed!) called the *mathematikoi*, which was like ancient Greece's version of a high school math club. The *mathematikoi* believed that numbers could unlock all the universe's secrets—from natural laws to poetry to music to philosophy. They didn't discover the Pythagorean theorem—the Indian mathematician Baudhayana wrote about it centuries before—but they did discover irrational numbers. A Pythagorean named Hippasus realized that the square root of 2 could not be expressed as a ratio of whole numbers. Unfortunately, this fact so upset Pythagoras that he had Hippasus executed, and then both the *mathematikoi* and mathematicians in general went ahead and pretended like irrational numbers didn't exist for more than a millennium.

Homer

The blind poet, whose epics *The Iliad* and *The Odyssey* are cornerstones of world literature and early examples of the use of figurative language, probably lived in the 8th century BCE—if, he lived at all, that is. So little is known about Homer that one prominent scholar argues that he was, in fact, a woman. Others think that Homer's poems were created by groups of people, while some argue there was a single poet whose words were modified by centuries of oral transmission.

Democritus (c. 450–370 BCE)

Democritus was a pre-Socratic philosopher who never gets any credit, even though he got things right a lot more often than most of his counterparts. Democritus was the first to argue, for instance, that all matter was made up of atoms (he wrongly thought atoms were indivisible, but hey, so did physicist Lord Kelvin 1,700 years later). Democritus also was the first to discover that the Milky Way was formed by light from distant stars (Aristotle, in his continuing attempts to be wrong about everything, later disagreed).

Herodotus (c. 484–425 BCE)

Herodotus is considered the first historian, in part because he coined the word *historie*, which had previously meant "inquiry." The documentarian's work focused on his travels and stories he'd heard, and his histories were primarily concerned with the lengthy conflict between Greece and the Persian Empire. But in those days before fact-checkers, Herodotus was wrong as often as he was right, and he often seemed more interested in telling a good story than a true one—for instance, Greek gods showed up in Herodotus's writing a lot more often than they tended to appear in real life. In fact, one historian argued that, in addition to being the "father of history," Herodotus was the "father of lies." We think that's a little harsh—we prefer "father of tabloid journalism."

Thucydides (c. 455–400 BCE)

Taking Herodotus's work one step further, Thucydides was the first historian to care about, well, telling the truth. Born into a wealthy and powerful family, Thucydides was living life high on the hog—he literally owned gold mines—until the Peloponnesian War broke out. Still a young man, Thucydides became a general. Through no fault of his own, his men failed to save a town from Spartan control, which led to Thucydides's exile for 20 years. But he spent the time well, writing *A History of the Peloponnesian War*, the world's first true history book. As research, Thucydides not only interviewed participants, but he read documents, and assiduously attempted to achieve objectivity in his work.

Quotable Ancient Greece

"Love is a serious mental disease."

—Plato

"One must not tie a ship to a single anchor, nor life to a single hope."

—Epicetus

"The unexamined life is not worth living."

—Socrates

"All I know is that I know nothing."

—Socrates

Hippocrates (c. 460–377 BCE)

Known in large part for his namesake oath, which is still recited by new physicians throughout the world, Hippocrates is often considered the greatest physician of all time—even though, for one thing, he did not write the Hippocratic Oath. In fact, some recent scholarship suggests the oath may have been written by some of Pythagoras's *mathematikoi*. For another thing, we're really glad that Hippocrates is not *our* doctor. His belief in the importance of balancing the four humors—phlegm, yellow bile, black bile, and blood—proved influential through the Middle Ages, although it wasn't influential in a decidedly positive direction (leeches were sometimes used to restore balance between the humors, for instance). But he was far less superstitious than his medical predecessors, was among the first to take a scientific approach to disease, emphasized the importance of cleanliness, and was the first physician to realize that thoughts and feelings begin in the brain, not the heart.

The Greek Alphabet

No self-respecting genius should be able to drive past a fraternity house and not pronounce its name, so here's the alphabet in order with upper and lowercase letters: Alpha (A, α), Beta (B, β), Gamma (Γ, γ), Delta (Δ, δ), Epsilon (E, ε), Zeta (Z, ζ), Eta (H, η), Theta (Θ, θ), Iota (I, ι), Kappa (K, κ), Lambda (Λ, λ), Mu (M, μ), Nu (N, ν), Xi (Ξ, ξ), Omicron (O, o), Pi (Π, π), Rho (P, ρ), Sigma (Σ, σ), Tau (T, τ), Upsilon (Y, υ), Phi (Φ, φ), Chi (X, χ), Psi (Ψ, ψ), Omega (Ω, ω).

PLAGIARIZE LIKE A GENIUS

T. S. Eliot once wrote, "Immature poets imitate; mature poets steal." And on your path to genius, it's likely you'll have to do some stealing of your own. Learn from, and take comfort in, the stories of these geniuses who managed to plagiarize with minimal damage to their reputations:

Samuel Taylor Coleridge—By T. S. Eliot's definition, Coleridge, the author of "Rime of the Ancient Mariner," was a very mature poet, indeed. In his book *Biographia Literaria*, Coleridge plagiarized extensively from several German philosophers, including Immanuel Kant, whose dense prose, we imagine, only *hurt* the quality of Coleridge's work. Coleridge also borrowed to the point of plagiarism in several of his poems.

George Harrison—Harrison's triple album *All Things Must Pass* is widely considered a masterpiece, and some say it's the best solo work by a former Beatle ever (sorry, Paul McCartney's *McCartney*). The song "My Sweet Lord" reached #1 in Britain twice—once upon its release in 1971 and again just after Harrison's death in 2002. But Harrison didn't get to enjoy the song's success either time. Striking similarities between Harrison's composition and the Chiffons' hit "He's So Fine" caused Harrison to be successfully sued for plagiarism, and he had to give up most of the royalties for the song. While the melodies are indeed very similar, the lyrics are somewhat different: "My Sweet Lord" is an invocation to God featuring references to the avatars of Vishnu, while "He's So Fine" is about—well, how fine he is.

Alex Haley—His epic novel *Roots* became a bestseller and was then adapted into the best TV miniseries ever. But it turned out that *Roots* had some illegitimate roots: Haley stole wide swaths of the book, word for word, from a book called *The African* by Harold Courlander. Haley ended up paying Courlander a whopping $650,000.

Helen Keller—When she was just 12 years old, blind and deaf Helen Keller—who'd overcome the odds to become literate—published a story called "The Frost King" in a small journal, which called Keller's story "without parallel in the history of literature." That turned out to be a somewhat inaccurate statement—Keller's story had many, many parallels to one by Margaret T. Canby called "The Frost Fairies." The plagiarism was deemed accidental, but Keller remained terrified of plagiarizing throughout her life.

Oscar Wilde

The playwright and wit Oscar Wilde was often accused of plagiarism, although nothing significant has ever been proven. Rarely did anyone ever out-banter Wilde, but one exception was a famous comment by James Whistler. After Whistler tossed off a good line, Wilde commented, "I wish I'd said that, James." Whistler answered, "Don't worry, Oscar. You will."

I5 ARTISTIC GENIUSES AND WHAT THEY DID THAT WAS SO FANCY

(or, why Pollack's paint splatters were genius and yours aren't—yet)

Botticelli

Sandro Botticelli's *The Birth of Venus* is one of the classics of Renaissance painting. But relatively few of Botticelli's works survive, because he fell into the most dangerous of all genius traps: He burned his work. (*See also* Kafka and Thomas Carlyle.) In middle age, Botticelli began attending a fire-and-brimstone church, which convinced him to abandon painting and throw much of his artwork into the fire.

Mary Cassatt

One of the few American impressionists, Cassatt was friends with the likes of Edgar Degas and Camille Pissarro. She was also one of the very few women to gain acceptance for her artwork in the 19th century. Cassatt never married and lived an atypical female life, but her work centered on mothers and children.

Willem de Kooning

The master of abstract expressionism (the art school in which, basically, the art is heavy on the action and light on the, uh, looking like something), De Kooning left the Netherlands at 22 to seek his fortune in America. He found it—by the end of his life, his works from the 1950s were selling for as much as $20 million.

Henri de Toulouse-Lautrec

Because of a genetic disorder, Toulouse-Lautrec's legs stopped growing when he was 14, leaving him with a normal-sized torso and head and very stubby legs. But that didn't stop the greatest art nouveau illustrator from playing the field. Toulouse-Lautrec often hung out at Le Moulin Rouge (John Leguizamo plays him in the eponymous movie)—and he knew a thing or two about the ladies of the cabaret: He died of syphilis at 36.

Vincent van Gogh

Van Gogh's long, hard life has been well-catalogued, but not always correctly retold: For one thing, Van Gogh didn't cut off his ear because he was heartbroken over a prostitute. He cut off *part* of his ear for the equally crazy reason that he'd just had a fight with Paul Gauguin. (He may or may not have given the ear to a prostitute.) Van Gogh sold no paintings in his lifetime, but today he's the world's most commercially successful 19th-century artist—his *Portrait of Dr. Gachet* sold for $82.5 million in 1990 (though its whereabouts are now unknown).

Auguste Rodin

Rodin was hugely prolific: He completed thousands of bronze sculptures, so many that two entire museums (one in Paris, the other in Philadelphia) are devoted solely to his work. But for all the variety, he is famous for exactly one piece: *The Thinker*, with its iconic chin-on-fist pose.

Ninja Turtles: a Helpful Chart

LEONARDO, THE NINJA TURTLE
Weapon of Choice: Katana swords
Favorite Color: Blue
Noted Achievements: Attaining leadership position among the Turtles; becoming Master Splinter's favorite protégé

LEONARDO, THE ARTIST
Weapon of Choice: Paint brush
Favorite Color: Fond of all of them, although from the way *The Last Supper* is deteriorating, we may not be able to appreciate his palette for long
Noted Achievements: *Mona Lisa* has done pretty well; also sketched inventions from submarines to helicopters to cluster bombs.

MICHELANGELO, THE NINJA TURTLE
Weapon of Choice: Nunchaku!
Favorite Color: Orange
Noted Achievements: Coined most of the Turtles' catchphrases, including "Cowabunga, dude!"

MICHELANGELO, THE ARTIST
Weapon of Choice: Marble and paintbrushes
Favorite Color: Flesh. Michelangelo loved him some nudity.
Noted Achievements: *David*; the ceiling of the Sistine Chapel

Rembrandt

Perhaps the most masterful of the old masters, Rembrandt specialized in the self-portrait. That makes sense, for two reasons. First, his work is considered thoughtful and introspective and

RAPHAEL, THE NINJA TURTLE

Weapon of Choice: Sai swords

Favorite Color: Red

Noted Achievements: The funniest Turtle. Also can throw a manhole cover like you read about.

RAPHAEL, THE ARTIST

Weapon of Choice: Paintbrush and pencil (the latter for his architecture)

Favorite Color: Lots of shades of brown

Noted Achievements: *The School of Athens; Portrait of Perugino*

DONATELLO, THE NINJA TURTLE

Weapon of Choice: Staff (Bo)

Favorite Color: Purple

Noted Achievements: The brains of the Turtles; inventor of Turtlevision.

DONATELLO, THE ARTIST

Weapon of Choice: Marble

Favorite Color: That marbly color

Noted achievements: Fewer than his counterparts, but his equestrian statue *Gattamelata* is quite famous.

deeply revealing of his subjects' humanness. And second, Rembrandt really, really liked himself. When he wasn't checking himself out in the mirror, Rembrandt painted everything from Biblical scenes (*Sacrifice of Isaac*) to images from contemporary life (*Anatomy Lesson of Dr. Nocolaes Tulp*).

Jackson Pollock

Known for the movie *Pollock* almost as much as his actual work, Jackson Pollock's troubled life made for a great film, but it's more fun watching a philandering alcoholic than it is being one (or being Pollock's wife, Lee Krasner, herself an important painter). So why are Pollock's splatter paintings so much better than those made by your 7-year-old? Pollock's drip paintings weren't random: They balance randomness and planning, and give off the energy that was inherent in their creation. Or that's what we're told, anyway.

Pablo Picasso

The brash Spanish painter who created Cubism and then outlasted it, Pablo Picasso was the anti–Van Gogh: He was rich, well-loved, and often giddily happy. He was even a minor movie star (his cameo appearances included Jean Cocteau's *Testament of Orpheus*). He was in fact so revered by his French countrymen that during the German occupation of Paris, the French Resistance smuggled Picasso bronze so he could work on his sculpture despite a German ban on his work. (One might argue that the French Resistance had more important things to focus on than the size of Picasso's bronze collection, but that's neither here nor there.)

Claude Monet

The first name in Impressionism, don't get Claude confused with his John Jacob Jingleheimer Smith, Edouard Manet. The artist responsible for the abundance of water lilies in every museum you ever visit, Monet's thick brushstrokes and obsession with correctly capturing light helped set him apart from other artists of his day. One other thing set him apart: While almost all the artists discussed here who were married cheated on their wives, only Monet brought his mistress to his wife's deathbed. It just goes to show—you don't have to be good to be a genius.

Eugène Delacroix

Unlike most of the painters who came before him, Delacroix didn't shy away from depicting suffering, and he often painted current events. His classic *Liberty Leading the People* showed a bare-breasted Liberty (who's nice-looking) holding the French flag and leading a band of peasant soldiers—some of whom are dead, and all of whom are not as nice-looking—to victory. (The French government bought the picture, but then didn't display it for a long time, on account of how King Louis Philippe was not, actually, all that keen on liberty.)

EXTREMELY SHORT SUMMARIES OF 31 WORKS OF LITERATURE

Goethe's Faust

What it is: A guy named Faust sells his soul to the devil in exchange for knowledge, and when he tries to get out of it, he learns that the devil gets his due. Nota bene: The author's name is pronounced GER-tuh.

Why it's important: For one thing, its plot has been copied time and again: *The Little Mermaid*, *Heathers*, and the song "Devil Went Down to Georgia" all bear some similarity to *Faust*—except they have happy endings.

Fyodor Dostoyevsky's Crime + Punishment

What it is: Poverty-stricken student Raskolnikov lives up to his rascally name by killing a pawnbroker and her sister, feels horrible about it, and then falls in love with a prostitute, who—as prostitutes go—seems quite a lot like a metaphor for God.

Why it's important: Perhaps Dostoyevsky's best-loved novel, it explores questions of suffering and salvation and isolation—all the great themes of the 19th century.

Leo Tolstoy's War & Peace

What it is: A huge cast of characters live and die during the Napoleonic era in Russia—probably the shortest summary you'll ever see of this 550,000-word novel.

Why it's important: Because there's simply no better work of historical fiction ever, and because it breaks so many novelistic conventions (the text includes nonfiction essays about the nature of war and history, for instance).

William Faulkner's Absalom, Absalom

What it is: Quentin Compson, at school at Harvard, tells his Canadian roommate the sad story of his Mississippi town, announcing in the end that he doesn't, doesn't, *doesn't hate* the South. (Quentin, needless to say, hates the South.)

Why it's important: One of the most daring and innovative American novels of the 20th century, it's also the best example of Faulkner's argument that "the past isn't dead; it's not even past."

James Joyce's Ulysses

What it is: Two men, a Jewish ad man named Leopold Bloom and a young would-be novelist named Stephen Dedalus, walk around Dublin on June 16, 1904, a day that lasts more than 1,000 pages.

Why it's important: Ulysses is endlessly layered and unprecedented in its ambitions. Many scholars rank it as the greatest literary achievement of the 20th century.

Thomas Hardy's Mayor of Casterbridge

What it is: Talk about the perils of drinking: After a fight with his wife, thoroughly soused 21-year-old Michael Henchard sells his wife and daughter to a sailor for the hefty sum of five guineas. Eighteen years later, Henchard is the thoroughly sober and well-respected mayor of Casterbridge when his wife reappears.

Why it's important: Hardy's lyrical descriptions of place and relentlessly tragic worldview combine brilliantly here, although some prefer the sexier *Jude the Obscure*, which was considered so raunchy in its day that booksellers sold it in brown paper bags.

Jane Austen's Emma

What it is: Rich, beautiful, and clever Emma decides to play matchmaker for not-rich, not-beautiful Harriet Smith, but things go wacky when Frank Churchill comes to town.

Why it's important: Austen's characters are extraordinarily well-drawn here—among the best in 19th-century literature—and, plus, the movie *Clueless* makes a lot more sense if you've read the book.

Mark Twain's The Adventures of Huckleberry Finn

What it is: Huck Finn, an irascible teenage river rat, rafts up the Mississippi with the slave Jim, meeting all sorts of interesting people on the way, including the School Board, who completely misunderstand Huck's adventure and promptly ban him.

Why it's important: As Hemingway put it, "All modern American literature comes from one book by Mark Twain called *Huckleberry Finn*." Nicely put, but it's *not* called *Huckleberry Finn*. (See above.)

J. D. Salinger's *Catcher in the Rye*

What it is: Holden Caulfield kicks around New York for a couple days after getting expelled from boarding school.

Why it's important: Love him for his pitch-perfect narrative voice or hate him for his cloying self-centeredness, Holden Caulfield has proven to be a favorite with both teenagers and John Lennon murderers.

Virginia Woolf's *To the Lighthouse*

What it is: A stream-of-consciousness novel that, insofar as it has a plot, is about a family's periodic trips to the Scottish Isle of Skye, which features a lighthouse that for complicated metaphorical reasons takes them more than a decade to actually visit.

Why it's important: Because it's a brilliant example of narration through interior monologue, and also because it's slightly more fun to read than other modernist masterpieces, like *Ulysses*.

Gabriel García-Márquez's *One Hundred Years of Solitude*

What it is: A fictional Colombian village called Macondo finds itself in the center of a century of Latin American history—from civil war to foreign investment to massacres to a kid being eaten to death by ants. Oh, right. That reminds us—like all of García Márquez's best novels, *Solitude* is a work of magical realism.

Why it's important: The best parable this side of Orwell's *Animal Farm*, this novel tells the story of Colombian history while simultaneously dealing with the complicated themes of time and narrative.

Chinua Achebe's Things Fall Apart

What it is: A wrestling champion and his three wives from an indigenous African community face the arrival of Christian missionaries.

Why it's important: Because its brief, metaphorically resonant story and pithy language make it that rare classic that's easy to read, and also because nothing before or since has captured the complex realities of colonialism in Africa.

Charles Dickens' A Tale of Two Cities

What it is: Ah, the French revolution—it was the best of times (in London), and it was the worst of times (in Paris). And it was particularly the worst of times for English lawyer Sydney Carton, who after a lifetime of cynicism makes a single act of sacrifice that—well, we don't want to spoil it for you—but it does involve the loss of a head.

Why it's important: Because even if you find Dickens a bit melodramatic here and there—and boy, do we—he is to be admired for his well-developed characters and intricate plots.

Jonathan Swift's Gulliver's Travels

What it is: This satiric attack on government and petty religious squabbles is also a parody of "travelers' tales," a possible genre in the 18th century. It is probably a hilarious parody, indeed, except no one ever reads travelers' tales anymore, and so doesn't get any of the jokes.

Why it's important: Because it's been continually in print for almost 300 years, for one thing—although we've always preferred Swift's "A Modest Proposal," the satiric essay in which he proposed eating Irish babies (many Brits of the day took him seriously).

Anonymous' Beowulf

What it is: In the old English classic, Beowulf, a great warrior, defeats a monster named Grendel. In the sequel, Beowulf, who is now a great king, defeats Grendel's mother—and then dies.

Why it's important: Mostly because it's the best work that has survived from the first millennium CE to be written in English— if you consider this to be English: ða se ellengæst earfoðlice þrage geþolode, se þe in þystrum bad, þæt he dogora gehwam dream gehyrde.

Geoffrey Chaucer's Canterbury Tales

What it is: A series of tales ("The Miller's Tale," "The Wife of Bath's Tale," etc.) about a group of pilgrims on their way to visit—get this—Canterbury. The stories are apparently outlandishly bawdy, if you can read Middle English.

Why it's important: It's one of the first books to be written in Middle English, rather than Latin or French, and because it's often seen, with *Beowulf*, as a cornerstone of pre-Shakespearean English literature.

Albert Camus' The Stranger

What it is: After shooting an Arab (*see also* The Cure's song "Killing an Arab"), Meursault is convicted of murder and, after a lot of first-person introspection, executed.

Why it's important: Written by the second-youngest writer ever to get the Nobel Prize, *The Stranger* is a classic of existentialism—which is a polysyllabic way of saying that 10th graders love it.

Mary Shelley's Frankenstein

What it is: With the help of some well-timed lightning, a doctor named Frankenstein creates a monster who is *not* named Frankenstein, despite what the sugary breakfast cereal Frankenberries seems to imply.

Why it's important: Because it's a still-relevant cautionary tale about the perils of amoral scientific exploration, and because it's possibly the first science fiction novel, and because reading it helps you to understand the monster in the classic video game *Castlevania*.

Franz Kafka's The Metamorphosis

What it is: A guy named Gregor wakes up one morning and discovers that he is a bug. And then, after a while as a bug, he dies.

Why it's important: It's an existential tragicomedy the likes of which we've never seen before—and it's open to more interpretations than Herman Melville's white whale.

F. Scott Fitzgerald's *The Great Gatsby*

What it is: It may just be the Great American Novel. The Great Gatsby is Jay Gatsby, a charming, self-made man who only hosts his lavish parties on West Egg island to attract the gorgeous, and married, Daisy.

Why it's important: Gatsby features economic prose, brilliant descriptions, and the best analysis of the American dream ever.

Vladimir Nabokov's *Lolita*

What it is: Humbert really, really likes Lolita, which is all fine and well until you consider that Lolita is 12.

Why it's important: Humbert's witty narration is full of word play and anagrams, and the tension between Humbert's European upbringing and his new American life says a lot about both continents.

Ralph Ellison's *Invisible Man*

What it is: A nameless narrator tells of his hard life spent in a basement apartment and on the streets of a city where everyone looks past him because of his skin color.

Why it's important: As complex as it is moving, the only novel Ellison published in his lifetime is one of the best novels ever written about the history of race in America.

Herman Melville's *Moby Dick*

What it is: Captain Ahab insists on chasing a massively metaphorical white whale named Moby Dick, until eventually everyone dies, except for me. Who am I? Just call me Ishmael.

Why it's important: The white whale, for one thing. Also, its interweaving of fact and fiction was revolutionary—although contemporary readers may grow weary of the ins and outs of 19th-century whale hunting.

Samuel Richardson's Clarissa

What it is: One of the longest novels ever published in English, the abridged version is 1,800 pages—so we'll just sum it up by saying it's about Clarissa, who has some romantic problems.

Why it's important: Because it is so incredibly long.

Marcel Proust's Remembrance of Things Past

What it is: A seven-volume coming-of-age novel about a guy who bears an uncanny resemblance to Marcel Proust.

Why it's important: Because its dense, complex, and rich language puts it alongside *Ulysses* as one of the greatest literary achievements of the 20th century. Also because the most popular American paperback edition weighs 7.2 pounds.

W.E.B. Du Bois' The Souls of Black Folk

What it is: A collection of Du Bois' brilliant essays on the role of race in America.

Why it's important: Because it's widely praised both for the quality of its language and for being one of the first great works of sociology.

Charlotte Brontë's Jane Eyre

What it is: Impoverished orphan Jane Eyre may not be much to look at, but she somehow manages to win over the handsome and rich Rochester, with whom she would live happily ever after—if only something could be done about the crazy lady locked in the attic.

Why it's important: Well, for one thing, because they, make a movie of it at least once a decade. There have been six already, including one in 1996 starring noted model/actress Elle Macpherson, who played history's most Australian-sounding Blanche Ingram.

Zora Neale Hurston's Their Eyes Were Watching God

What it is: Janie Crawford, the granddaughter of a slave, tells the story of her three marriages and in doing so captures and analyzes the lives of African Americans in the post–Civil War era.

Why it's important: Because it is an excellent collection of folklore incomparably written, and because it has a great first line: "Ships at a distance have every man's wish onboard."

Ernest Hemingway's For Whom the Bell Tolls

What it is: An American soldier fighting in the Spanish Civil War falls for a girl, which makes him think twice about his death wish.

Why it's important: Because it tolls for thee, man.

Miguel Cervantes' Don Quixote

What it is: In history's first real buddy comedy, a crazy guy named Don Quixote bums around Spain with his sidekick, Sancho Panza. Together, they right some wrongs, ride a hilariously skinny horse, and tilt at windmills.

Why it's important: First published in 1605, it's the first real novel of any literary consequence.

Nathaniel Hawthorne's
The Scarlet Letter

What it is: A woman who already has the misfortune of being named Hester has the further misfortune of engaging in non-marital sexual contact in her Puritan town, after which she is forced to wear clothes emblazoned with a scarlet A.

Why it's important: The Puritans had been gone for a century by the time Hawthorne got around to writing about them, but the novel is still a damning indictment of religious hypocrisy—past, present, and future.

Congratulations! You are now half-way to full-fledged Genius.

At this point, you're basically the indubitably brilliant Nikola Tesla—or at least half of him, anyway. We'll say his head, arms, and torso—all the parts that did the hard work. Being as smart as Tesla means that you're well-equipped to make tremendous breakthroughs in the field of electromagnetism. But it also means that, like Tesla, you're not quite smart enough to remember to patent your work. And because you don't, you end up living in a series of low-rent hotels in New York City in your final years, and your only friends will be pigeons. Plus, you'll repeatedly be beaten out for the Nobel Prize by a series of scientists far inferior to you. On the other hand, you might get a five-piece guitar-heavy hair band named after you, so life isn't too bad.

SOME ECONOMIC LAWS TO KNOW

The laws of supply and demand are the theoretical basis for most analysis of free market economies. Let's begin with demand, because it's moody and gets cranky if we start with supply. Economists don't define demand as merely wanting something; demand involves not only 1. desire, but also 2. the ability to pay and 3. the willingness to pay. (We, for instance, would theoretically like a puppy, but then we start to think about all the responsibilities involved, and we decide that we aren't willing to pay for the privilege of buying a lot of carpet cleaner as well.) When all three conditions are not met, the demand is called "not real." (Seriously. They aren't a terribly creative lot, these economists.)

The law of demand states, "Quantity demanded is inversely proportional to price." That is, as prices go down, real demand goes up. When demand far exceeds supply in a free market, scarcity causes prices to skyrocket, which is the only possible explanation for the fact that in December of 1996, some Tickle Me Elmo dolls sold for thousands of dollars.

The law of supply dictates, "Quantity supplied is directly proportional to price." That is, the more the price of Tickle Me Elmo dolls go up, the more Tickle Me Elmo dolls will be produced.

Well, in a theoretically pure market economy, anyway. In real life, sometimes it's just not possible to produce enough Tickle Me Elmo dolls before Christmas, due to constraints of production.

When you put in graphed supply and demand curves together, they meet at the fair market price for an item.

So the fair market price for a velvet Elvis painting ends up at one thin dime. Sorry, Elvis. Don't blame us. That's just the free market at work.

Diminishing Returns

The law of diminishing marginal returns asserts that a continuing increase in input yields a smaller and smaller increase in output. That is, if you own a 10-acre giant beanstalk farm, and you plant 100 magic seeds, you might end up with, say, 100 giant beanstalks. If you plant 200 seeds, though, you may not have time to tend them all, and the plants may crowd each other for sun and water and root space. So you won't end up with 200 giant beanstalks, but maybe 170. And so on, until eventually you're throwing a lot of magic seeds into the ground for a very minimal increase in gigantic beanstalks, making it a poor investment.

WAR: 9 BATTLEFIELD GENIUSES AND WHAT THEY CAN TEACH YOU

Sun-Tzu

The Experience: A Chinese general who probably lived in the 4th century BCE, very little is known about Sun Tzu's wartime exploits—but he wrote *The Art of War*, the best war strategy book ever.

The Lessons: *The Art of War*'s advice on maneuvering large armies and varying tactics has been used by everyone from Mao Zedong to Napoleon.

Quote to Carry with You into Battle: "If you know your enemies and know yourself, you will not be imperiled in 100 battles."

Simón Bolívar (1783–1830)

The Experience: The George Washington of South America, *el libertador* fought for the independence of Venezuela, Colombia, Ecuador, Peru, Panama, and the not-coincidentally-named Bolivia. But Bolívar proved a better general than a politician: Internal strife forced him out of all leadership roles in his newly independent nations shortly before his death in 1830.

The Lessons: It's easier to conquer land than it is to rule it.

Quote to Carry with You into Battle: "The art of victory is learned in defeat."

Alexander the Great (356–323 BCE)

The Experience: Probably the greatest general ever, Alexander's empire stretched from his native Greece to the Nile to the Punjab. That's a particularly remarkable accomplishment when you consider that he died at 32.

The Lessons: Be nice to your own army, and be really, really mean to everyone else. (When Alexander's second-in-command and possible lover Hephaestion died, for instance, Alexander reportedly had Hephaestion's attending physician crucified for malpractice.)

Quote to Carry into Battle: "I would not fear a pack of lions led by a sheep, but I would always fear a flock of sheep led by a lion."

Genghis Khan (c. 1162–1227)

The Experience: Genghis Khan founded the Mongol Empire, which at its height included China, most of the former Soviet Union, and a fair bit of central Europe. An adherent of the "raping and pillaging" school of warfare, Genghis Khan *really* enjoyed killing.

The Lessons: Superior tactics can beat superior firepower. Genghis was famous for his faked retreats and for finding ways to force his enemies to fight on two fronts.

Quote to Carry into Battle, Which We Swear Is Not Made Up: "The greatest happiness is to vanquish your enemies, to chase them before you, to rob them of their wealth, to see those dear to them bathed in tears, to clasp to your bosom their wives and daughters." (Yikes.)

Julius Caesar (100–44 BCE)

The Experience: A god to the Romans (literally), just one of whose wars resulted in, according to a Roman historian, 800 conquered cities, 3 million enemy dead, and 1 million new slaves. He came and saw and conquered, indeed. Unfortunately for Caesar, he was later assassinated by a guy named Brutus, as in *"Et tu, Brute."*

The Lessons: Beware the Ides of March. Also, beware disloyal and power-hungry underlings.

Quote to Carry into Battle: Upon crossing the river Rubicon to begin the Roman Civil War of 49 BCE, Caesar coined the phrase, "The die is cast." Not a bad line to use in any ominous situation.

Nelson Mandela (1918–)

The Experience: Although he won the Nobel Peace Prize and is generally seen as an example of pacifistic civil disobedience, Mandela was head of the African National Congress's Spear of the Nation, a group that planned guerrilla warfare attacks and sabotage against the Apartheid government.

The Lessons: This is one case where the pen was actually mightier than the sword. Mandela's writings from prison did much more to end apartheid than Spear of the Nation ever accomplished.

Quote to Carry into Battle: During his trial in 1963, Mandela said, "I planned [sabotage] as a result of a calm and sober assessment of the political situation. Without violence there would be no way open to the African people to succeed in their struggle."

Ulysses S. Grant (1822–1885)

The Experience: Upon taking control of the better equipped but poorly led Union army in 1864, Grant outmaneuvered Robert E. Lee and finally brought an end to the Civil War. He then went on to become one of America's worst, and drunkest, presidents.

The Lessons: With a lot more troops, a lot more natural resources, better weapons, and more money, you will generally win.

Quote to Carry into Battle: "The art of war is simple enough. Find out where your enemy is. Get at him as soon as you can. Strike him as hard as you can, and keep moving."

Geronimo (1829–1909)

The Experience: Despite the rumors that his name means "One who yawns," Geronimo's life was a heckuva ride: He led the last Apache army to surrender to the United States, battling for three decades, until he and his last 38 followers were finally captured in 1886.

The Lesson: With fewer troops, fewer natural resources, lesser weapons, and less money, you will generally lose.

Quote to Carry into Battle: "[God] created all tribes of men and certainly had a righteous purpose in creating each."

Napoléon (1769–1821)

The Experience: Known as the Little Corporal, Bonaparte became famous by mowing down protestors on the streets of Paris with high-powered artillery. He went on to become emperor of France and generally a huge fan of himself.

The Lesson: Never invade Russia in the wintertime. This is one of those lessons that despots have learned over and over again (*see also* Hitler).

Quote to Carry into Battle: " 'Impossible' is not a word in French." (This is technically untrue. The French word for impossible is *impossible*.)

MODERNISM VS. POSTMODERNISM

Here's a rule of thumb: If it happened before, or during, or just after World War I, it's definitely modernism. If it happened before or during World War II, it's *probably* still modernism. And if it has happened since, it's probably postmodernism. But things get murky when you try to specifically address the difference between the two words, for one simple reason: Deep down in their hearts, no one really knows exactly what the word *postmodernism* means. In fact, whenever you hear people say the word *postmodern*, you should innocently ask what exactly they mean by that, and then watch them fumble.

But to begin, let's just take it literally. *Post*modernism is that which came after *modernism*. The cultural movement of modernism originated, of course, in France—whose chief exports over the years have been wine, cheese, and cultural movements. In the mid-19th century, everything Europe had agreed upon for centuries—Christianity, Newtonian physics, the health benefits of getting your blood sucked out by leeches—was being called into question. Darwin was questioning our presumptions about human origins; Marx was railing against the free market economy; problems with Newton's laws were becoming more vexing; the French were beginning to wonder if maybe they should have an emperor *not* named Napoléon; et cetera.

At first, it was known as the *avant-garde*—with poets like Baudelaire and painters like Manet at the forefront. But by the 1890s, everyone was jumping on the modernism bandwagon. Soon, a mix of alienation and inquisitiveness had spread throughout the arts. Should music sound pretty? Maybe not, argued the atonal compositions of Schoenberg. Should paintings look like stuff? Heck no, said the likes of Kandinsky and Picasso. Most of the artists we think of as 20th-century geniuses are considered modernists: from James Joyce to T. S. Eliot to Federico García Lorca to Gertrude Stein to Le Corbusier to Cézanne.

With company like that, you'd think everyone would be content just to keep the modernism party jumping. But modernism became the lower-back tattoo of cultural movements: At first, it seemed revolutionary; then, for a while, it was popular but still excitingly dangerous; and then it was so popular that it became kinda lame. Enter postmodernism, stage left.

As an artistic reaction to modernism, postmodernism has

Mo + Pomo, Exemplified

LITERATURE
Modern: *The Great Gatsby*
Straddling the Fence: *Ulysses*
Postmodern: *Lolita*

MUSIC
Modern: Schoenberg's *Five Pieces for Orchestra*
Straddling the Fence: Edgard Varèse's *Ionisation* (the first piece to feature solely percussion, thus presaging the decidedly pomo Blue Man Group)
Postmodern: John Cage's *4'33"* (which is 4 minutes and 33 seconds of silence)

ARCHITECTURE
Modern: Frank Lloyd Wright's houses
Straddling the Fence: There is no fence-straddling in architecture!
Postmodern: Ricardo Legorreta's San Antonio Public Library

been defined by ideas like self-conscious deconstructive literature (exploring the ways in which meaning is constructed using text). Some say the first postmodern line in literature comes in the final chapter of Joyce's modernist masterpiece *Ulysses*, when Joyce has the character Molly Bloom announce, "O Jamesy let me up out of this." This acknowledgment of the author's existence in a work of fiction is distinctly postmodern, as is multimedia art, and the tension between high art and low culture (see, for instance, the Dadaist Marcel Duchamp putting a urinal in a gallery and calling it art).

> **ART**
> Modern: Picasso's *Guernica*
> Straddling the Fence:
> Salvador Dalí's *The Disintegration of the Persistence of Memory*
> Postmodern: Robert Rauschenberg's *Erased de Kooning Drawing* (which is—you guessed it—a de Kooning drawing that Rauschenberg erased and then put on display)

60%

genius

Congratulations! You are now 60% of the way toward full-fledged Genius.

If you were a political genius, right now you'd be James K. Polk, America's 11th president. That is to say, you're undoubtedly brilliant. First, you surprise even yourself by winning the election of 1844 on the strength of your charisma and your humble promise to serve only one term. Second, you're quite a good president. You acquire more than a million square miles of new territory for the United States (sorry, Mexico), oversee the opening of the Washington Monument, and issue the very first American postage stamps! So yes, no doubt. You're well on your way to true political genius. But you still have a little to learn: For one thing, you *keep your promise* to serve only one term, whereas the true political genius would serve at least three (see, for instance, Franklin Delano Roosevelt). Furthermore, you still haven't learned the manifest benefits of relentless self-promotion: Your humility has often left you over-looked on historians' lists of first-rate presidents.

GLOBAL WARMING

One of the biggest keys to genius is solving a big problem: Jonas Salk would never have become famous without the scourge of polio; Abraham Lincoln needed the Civil War to establish his leadership genius; without forest fires, Smokey the Bear would never have risen to prominence. Fortunately, there are a number of big, unsolved problems remaining, and global warming is fast shaping up to be near the top.

Global warming is a hugely controversial subject, particularly for something that reasonably ought to be solvable just by looking at a thermometer. Scientists fall into three broad camps:

> 1. The vast majority of climatologists believe in anthropogenic global warming; i.e., that it's our fault. Increased release of carbon dioxide, methane, and other "greenhouse gases" due primarily to the burning of fossil fuels has led to an increase in the "greenhouse effect." The effect, which was discovered in 1924 and occurs regardless of whether you drive a Hummer, is the process by which gases such as carbon dioxide and methane function as greenhouse

walls in the atmosphere, keeping solar warmth near Earth. Scientists estimate that without the natural level of greenhouse gases, global temperatures would drop 30 degrees—so keep breathing, because your exhalations are an important source of carbon dioxide. The problem with your Hummer is that it's drastically increasing the amount of greenhouse gases released into the atmosphere, which magnifies the greenhouse effect. That warms the earth too much, which may or may not eventually result in drought, hurricanes, and all that *The Day After Tomorrow* stuff.

2. A few scientists believe that global warming *isn't* caused by humanity at all, but is just part of the natural warming of the earth.

3. Even fewer scientists believe that the earth actually *isn't* warming at all, but that (seriously) the thermometers are all wrong. In a related story, some scientists believe that no one can see you if you stick your head in the sand.

The UN has stated that at current rates of growth, the average temperature on earth will increase between 2.5 and 10.5 degrees Fahrenheit between 1990 and 2100, which could melt enough of the polar ice cap to make New York City America's Venice. The effect might not be that dramatic, of course, which is one of the problems with climate research: Because warming rates like this have never been seen before, it's nearly impossible to predict what will really happen. Hopefully, we won't have to find out, because (fingers crossed) you or one of your fellow newly minted geniuses will find a way to slow global warming.

What's that you say? For starters, we could just adopt smaller, more fuel-efficient cars? Oh, come on, Dreamy McHeadinthe-clouds. We need a *realistic* solution.

Tuvalu

There is, perhaps, no one in the world more concerned about global warming than Maatia Toafa, the prime minister of the Pacific island nation of Tuvalu. Toafa could be out of a job shortly, because his nation may soon cease to exist. At its highest point, Tuvalu is all of 6½ feet above sea level, meaning that technically it would be better off sitting on Shaquille O'Neal's shoulders. But Tuvaluans should be thankful their nation has at least hung around long enough to participate in the Internet economy: Almost half of Tuvalu's GDP comes from the lease of its sweet domain name, .tv.

HOW TO DRESS LIKE A LEFT-BRAINED GENIUS

You will notice, first, that you are dressed as a woman. There are three reasons for this: First, many left-brained geniuses are women (chemist Marie Curie, mathematician Maria Agnesi). Second, many experts believe that the reason there aren't *more* female left-brained geniuses is a general bias against women in the sciences. And we here at **mental**_floss are all about empowering women to excel. And third, you look great in that skirt, little lady.

Most left-brained geniuses don't wear lab coats to work, but you're probably going to have to become accustomed to the touch, the feel of latex—as it's gonna be the fabric of your life. Why? Well, so you don't end up like Marie Curie, who won Nobel Prizes in physics *and* chemistry (and bore a daughter who won the chemistry prize in 1930). Curie's untimely death from leukemia was probably caused by her bad habit of playing around with enriched uranium barehanded.

If you're trying to look like a left-brained genius, head to the salon and get yourself a 'do with some body. From Albert Einstein's frizz to Isaac Newton's rolling, girlish curls to Werner Heisenberg's gelled-up flat-top, left-brained geniuses want their hair like they want their ideas: Big, revolutionary, and a little crazy.

ECCENTRIC GENIUS OR JUST PLAIN CRAZY?

Aristotle said, "No excellent soul is exempt from a mixture of madness." So if you want to be perceived as an excellent soul, it makes sense to mix a little madness in for kicks. But you can't take it too far. To help keep you steady on that tricky balance beam of sanity, here's a guide to those who managed to stay weirdly brilliant, and those who went completely nuts:

Friedrich Nietzsche

The Case for Genius: Philosophy books like *The Will to Power* and *Beyond Good and Evil* are still staples of collegiate philosophy classes. He inspired the existentialist thinkers who came after him, and challenged all our preconceived notions about morality.

The Case for Crazy: In 1889, Nietzsche was discovered in hysterics, hugging a horse. It was the beginning of a nervous breakdown from which he never recovered, living as an invalid the rest of his life. Some have argued his illness was caused by syphilis, which begs the question: Who *didn't* have syphilis in 19th-century Europe?

The Verdict: ECCENTRIC GENIUS. His final insanity never really marred his reputation.

Howard Hughes

The Case for Genius: Hughes directed or produced several hit movies in the 20s and 30s, but his real genius lay in aeronautical engineering: He designed and flew the H-1 Racer, which set a world speed record for aircraft in 1935, and built the humongous Spruce Goose almost entirely out of wood.

The Case for Crazy: Hughes suffered from obsessive-compulsive disorder (he also had syphilis, but that's neither here nor there). He only trimmed his nails once a year, stored his urine in jars, wore Kleenex boxes as shoes, had the windows of his hotel room blacked out, and would sort his peas by size before beginning to eat them. In short, he was . . .

The Verdict: JUST PLAIN CRAZY.

Beethoven

The Case for Genius: In spite of ever-worsening hearing, Beethoven composed several of the most recognizable symphonies in history and, perhaps most importantly, lent his name to a lovable St. Bernard in the iconic films *Beethoven*, *Beethoven's 2nd*, and *Beethoven's 3rd*.

The Case for Crazy: Beethoven often walked the streets of Vienna dressed in rags and muttering to himself and was known for his childish outbursts. It turns out that some of this odd behavior might be attributable to lead poisoning, which probably caused his death. Regardless, he was unquestionably an . . .

Our Verdict: ECCENTRIC GENIUS.

Jack Kerouac

The Case for Genius: Kerouac wrote one widely admired novel, *On the Road*, in three weeks—thanks to the help of coffee and amphetamines.

The Case for Crazy: Kerouac's last decades were marked by literary failure alcoholism, drug abuse, bouts of manic violence, and crushing depression.

Our Verdict: JUST PLAIN CRAZY. There's a lesson here, future literary geniuses: You might write *one* great novel hopped up on speed, but that's no way to build a career. He would never repeat this feat of "spontaneous prose."

NUCLEAR REACTIONS

There are two varieties of nuclear reaction: fission and fusion. In terms of pure science, nuclear fission occurs when an atomic nucleus is split into two or more smaller nuclei. Meanwhile, a nuclear chain reaction occurs only in extremely heavy isotopes of a few elements. These isotopes give off neutrons during the fission process *and* undergo fission when hit by a neutron, meaning that they can create a self-sustaining chain reaction. When this happens inside a nuclear reactor, it can result in cheap and bountiful energy to the world. When it happens inside a nuclear bomb, it can result in Hiroshima.

But, as nuclear reactions inside bombs go, fission is certainly preferable to its counterpart. Fusion, of course, is the process through which two or more nuclei are fused together. In certain nuclei, fusion results in the absorption of energy, but in certain isotopes of lighter elements, such as hydrogen, fusion releases a tremendous amount of energy—enough to produce the catastrophic effects of a hydrogen bomb. But fusion is far from easy to achieve. Nuclei are like Montana hermits: They don't really like to come into contact with one another, and they certainly don't want to form a lasting union. The only way devised so far to overcome this natural repulsion is to create a tremendous

How Hard Is It to Make a Nuclear Bomb?

We can't really think of any noncriminal reason why you'd ask that question, but we're happy to answer it anyway. It's pretty hard; you certainly couldn't do it without a sophisticated laboratory. The first thing you need to do is heat your uranium until it becomes a liquid, which will cause some gas to steam off. Then you enrich the uranium by pumping that gas through a series of porous membrane filters. Then condense the gas back into a li—wait a second. There are a few things even geniuses don't need to know, so we're just going to stop right there.

amount of energy. In the case of modern fusion bombs, this is usually accomplished by having a small fission bomb go off *inside* the larger fusion bomb, which gives off enough energy to lead to fusion.

Most of the nuclear reactions we know (and fear) today involve fission, not fusion. Although scientists have been trying for decades to build über-powerful fusion reactors, none has yet succeeded at creating energy. (Well, there is one fusion reactor on which we rely: the sun. But other than that, all nuclear energy comes from fission.)

And when people express anxiety about rogue states developing nuclear weapons, they almost always mean fission bombs. Hiroshima and Nagasaki were catastrophic examples of the power of a fission bomb, but they're still far preferable to their fusion counterparts: Commonly known as hydrogen bombs, some fusion bombs are hundreds of times more powerful than the weapons dropped on Japan in 1945. Fortunately, fusion bombs are also more complicated than their counterparts—unless one is stolen, it's unlikely rogue states will be developing them anytime soon.

BINARY NUMERAL SYSTEM: BECAUSE EVERY COMPUTER GENIUS KNOWS THE ABC'S, THE 123'S, AND THE 010'S.

These days, almost all people in the world use the base-10 number system (i.e., we use 10 symbols in calculations: 0, 1, 2, 3, 4, 5, 6, 7, 8, and 9). Think of base-10 as the Windows of numerical systems: Sure, it's the most popular, but it's hardly the only option. Douglas Adams' *The Restaurant at the End of the Universe*, for instance, which asserts that the meaning of life is the number 42, refers to a base-13 counting system. Or, for a more practical application, using a base-4 numeral system allows scientists to represent the four nucleotides of DNA numerically.

But by far the most popular non-base-10 number system is binary, which involves just two symbols, 1 and 0. In the future, when a robotic Arnold Schwarzenegger comes to save you from the robots because you are humanity's greatest genius and must be preserved at all costs, all the bad guys trying to kill you won't be counting in base-10. They'll be using binary, just like computers.

Binary works for computers because it's easy to use within electronic circuits, since there are only two possible outcomes: 0 and 1. This makes for some funny-looking math. For instance, in binary, $1 + 1 = 10$, which is the kind of fact that can potentially win you a bet at a bar, so it's worth taking a closer look:

Funny Ha-Ha

Having completed your introduction to binary, test yourself by seeing if you laugh at the world's best (and possibly only) binary joke: "There are 10 kinds of people in the world: Those who understand binary, and those who don't."

In base-10 counting, the digits in a number increase when you go one step past nine, i.e., a two-digit number (10) follows the highest one-digit number (9). The same rule holds in binary, only there are only two numbers. So after 0 comes 1, and after 1 comes 10, and after 10 comes 11, and then 100, 101, 111, 1000, 1001, 1011, etc. If, for some reason, you find the need to count *out loud* in binary (hey, it helps us), you should pronounce each digit: 100 is not "a hundred," but "one zero zero."

You can also count on your hands using binary: Simply raise a finger for 1, and lower it for 0. (Note: Choose the finger wisely.)

PATRON GENIUSES II: ELECTRIC(ITY) BOOGALOO

Patron Genius of Pigeons

Nikola Tesla, who proved the superiority of alternating current and whose ideas were regularly borrowed by the likes of Thomas Edison and George Westinghouse, had a pretty rough go of it: He never married and had few friends. Well, human friends, anyway. But he really loved pigeons—and not in the sweet, harmless way that the more sane among us might love pigeons. Of one particular white pigeon, he said, "I loved her as a man loves a woman, and she loved me."

The Patron Genius of Lost Loves

André-Marie Ampère. Also the patron genius of guys with the middle name Marie, Ampère is famous for his discovery of electromagnetism—the unit of measure for electric currency was later named the ampere. But all his discoveries gave him very little joy—he remained more or less permanently bereft after his wife Julie died in her late 20s.

Sparky McSparksalot

If there was one historical character who needed the prayers of Ben Franklin, it was Virginian forest ranger **Roy "Sparky" Sullivan.** Between 1942 and 1977 Sparky was struck by lightning a world-record *seven* times. Forgive us, but: He was positively electric. Sullivan survived all seven strikes, but then committed suicide in 1983, reportedly over a love affair gone sour, proving once and for all that Zeus's lightning is no match for the sting of Cupid's arrow. (The odds of getting struck by lightning seven times, incidentally, are in the neighborhood of 1 in 64,339,296,875,000,000,000,000,000,000,000.)

The Patron Genius of Those Struck by Lightning

Although *Benjamin Franklin's* kite-in-a-lightning-storm experiment is the stuff of American legend, it may never have happened. Some speculate that Franklin never *really* flew a kite in a lightning storm, or that he proved there was static electricity in the air without getting struck by lightning (others who tried the kite trick ended up dead). Regardless, Franklin gets Patron Genius over lightning victims, thanks to his invention of the lightning rod.

The Patron Genius of Dead Frogs

You may think the world has no need for a patron genius of dead frogs, but little Lucy's going to need *someone* to turn to when her adorable little Mr. Ribbit goes to the great lilypad in the sky. And there's no finer candidate than *Luigi Galvani,* who one day noticed the leg of a very dead frog twitching whenever his steel scalpel touched a brass hook holding the frog's legs. Resurrection! Well, not really.

TIMELINE: EUREKA! MOMENTS TO REMEMBER

c. 240 BCE: The original Eureka! moment: Greek scientist Archimedes, frustrated with his inability to figure out a way to measure density, decides to take a bath. Climbing into the tub, he notices the water level go up, and realizes that water displacement can be used to determine density and buoyancy. And then, being the kind of genius who quietly and humbly celebrates his discoveries, Archimedes jumps out of the bath and runs stark naked through the streets of Syracuse shouting *Eureka!* ("I found it!")

1641: Even the finest European clocks are unreliable, gaining and losing time seemingly at whim. The blind, 77-year-old Galileo Galilei recalls seeing a lamp swing in the cathedral of Pisa when he was a student and realizes that pendulums could be harnessed to regulate clocks. Since he's blind, his sketches aren't that great—but still, Galileo becomes the grandfather of the grandfather clock.

c. 1666: Sir Isaac Newton is sitting in his mother's garden in Cambridge, England, when he notices an apple fall from a tree (no vaguely reliable source ever claimed it hit him on the head). All of a sudden, Newton realizes that the same force that brings the apple to the ground holds the moon in orbit around the earth. Great story, but it may not be true: The apple tale was popularized by Voltaire half a century later, and some think Voltaire made it up to make Newton seem like more of a rationalist.

c. 1742: Six-year-old James Watt is absolutely obsessed with tea kettles, pondering such important questions as: What makes them whistle? How does the steam produce enough force to push open the lid? And why does Mommy look like a zombie in the morning until she has her caffeinated tea? Twenty-three years later, Watt builds the first of his famed steam engines.

1820: In a Eureka! moment that inexorably leads to the trinity of evil that is disco, spandex, and Speedos, Thomas Hancock comes up with a machine that can produce elastic.

1844: A Eureka! moment you're glad you didn't have: Vermont dentist Horace Wells attends a "Laughing Gas Show" (the 19th-century whip-it party) featuring nitrous oxide. Wells realizes laughing gas could lessen the pain of tooth extraction. He organizes a demonstration, but a mechanical problem prevents the nitrous from working. Humiliated, Wells goes completely bonkers. He sells his dental practice, leaves his wife and family, starts anesthetizing himself a bit too much, and then begins hurling sulfuric acid at the faces of prostitutes. That gets him jailed, where Wells becomes addicted to chloroform and, in 1848, commits suicide by, uh, cutting his groin (to put it politely).

1848: Sawmill operator James Marshall, working in Sutter's Mill, discovers several gold nuggets near Coloma, California.

1855: In a somewhat more literal Eureka! moment, Eureka College is founded in Eureka, Illinois.

1886: Wealthy Illinoisan Josephine Cochrane, tired of her servants breaking dishes while trying to wash them, invents the first dishwasher.

1897: Researcher Felix Hoffmann discovers a way to make a safe derivative of the toxic but fever-reducing salicylic acid. Hoffmann gives the drug to his arthritic father, who reports it is miraculous. Aspirin, the first genuinely synthetic drug, goes on to treat everything from fever to heart attacks.

1897: Exactly eleven days later, the very same Felix Hoffmann invents a synthesized version of morphine, which he calls heroin.

1948: After a walk through the Swiss Alps, engineer Georges de Mestral finds dozens of burdock seeds sticking to his clothing. "Hey," he thinks. "I could use this to invent Velcro, and then one day people wearing Velcro suits will trampoline into walls covered in Velcro wallpaper." (Or something like that.) And so it comes to pass.

1990: During a delay-ridden, four-hour train trip between Manchester and London, Jo Rowling gets an idea for a book about a scrawny prodigy at a wizard school.

ROCKET SCIENCE
IN A NUTSHELL

It's the ultimate test of a left-brained genius. But rocket science isn't just for rocket scientists anymore! As it turns out, rocket science isn't all that complicated. The difference between a rocket and, say, a Volkswagen Rabbit is that our *rocket* doesn't break down nearly every week. Wait, no, the difference between rockets and other engines is that rockets can be used in the vacuum of space, because unlike jet engines, rockets don't need to suck in air, and unlike car engines, they don't require a fluid fuel medium.

Rockets come in many varieties, but from space shuttles to bottle rockets, they all work by expelling gases in the direction opposite their motion. It all goes back to Newton's Third Law of Motion: For every action, there is an equal and opposite reaction. Put in rocket science terms: The more momentum carried away by the exhaust, the faster the rocket goes in the opposite direction. The high-speed exhaust is achieved first by a combustion reaction inside a chamber. The gas is then allowed to escape through the rocket's narrow throat, and then into a cone-shaped nozzle (picture the bottom of a space shuttle), which accelerates the mass and velocity of the exhaust. Liftoff.

The job of every rocket scientist is to make a rocket engine that allows the rocket to provide a lot of thrust without, well, blowing up. And this, as it happens, is the real difficulty, because the massively combustible propellants needed to really get a rocket scooting tend toward blowing up, which is one of several reasons why you should be glad you didn't pilot Germany's experimental rocket-engine aircraft during World War II.

As for their history, rockets have been around for centuries. In fact, they were used as weapons in China going back to at least the 1200s. The earliest rockets are now known as "solid rockets" because they contained solid propellants, like gunpowder. But pretty much all rocket fuels contain an oxidizer and a fuel. In gunpowder, charcoal is the fuel and potassium nitrate is the oxidizer. In contemporary solid rocket engines, such as the booster rockets that provide most of the space shuttle's initial acceleration, the fuels and oxidizers are more complicated mixes—but the same basic principle is at work.

If you've ever tried to reuse a bottle rocket, you'll already know the downside of a solid rocket. Once they start burning, they can't stop. Liquid propellants, on the other hand, are able to be turned on and off, and even throttled, which makes them vital if you want to regulate your speed in, say, space. When using liquid propellants, separate chambers store the oxidizers and fuels, and then they're pumped into a combustion chamber, where they become rocket fuel. The disadvantage of liquid propellants is that oxidizers are difficult to come by: Nitric acids are extremely toxic, for instance, and liquid oxygen has to be kept very cold. Still, many rocket engines now use primarily liquid propellants, including those inside American ICBM missiles and orbiting satellites.

So next July 4th, when your spouse and/or the long arm of the law is complaining about your ultra-high-quality bottle rocket displays (all fireworks, incidentally, use solid propellants), you can now technically defend yourself by saying, "Well, I *have* studied rocket science."

70%

genius

Congratulations! You are now 70% of the way toward full-fledged Genius.

At this point, you're in what we like to call "Christopher Marlowe limbo." Like the British poet and playwright Marlowe (1564–1593), you are indisputably gifted. Marlowe, after all, has been in print more than 400 years, which isn't a bad record at all. And his translation of Ovid's *Elegies* is still admired. But he will always live in the shadow of that fellow across town by the name of Shakespeare. If you want to achieve true unadulterated genius, you must press on past the Marlowe limbo. Really, you *must*. Otherwise, you might get knifed in a fight and die before your 30th birthday, as Marlowe did.

HOW TO GO CRAZY
LIKE A GENIUS

One of the disadvantages to becoming a genius is that your chances of going crazy skyrocket. Several scientific studies have shown that a significant link between right-brained genius and mental illness exists, particularly major depressive disorders. To supplement such studies, we gathered together this entirely unscientific overview:

Obsessive-Compulsive Disorder

What It Is: An anxiety disorder that most commonly shows itself in obsessive thoughts and compulsive actions. This may mean an inability to stop worrying about acquiring a disease, for instance. To make the obsession go away, a person might compulsively wash his or her hands. (Indeed, some OCD sufferers wash their hands hundreds of times a day.)

Geniuses Afflicted: Charles Dickens was obsessively tidy, always needed his bed aligned in a north-south position, and habitually touched objects three times for luck. Lexicographer and author Samuel Johnson counted his steps and, like many OCD sufferers today, had complicated rituals surrounding walking through doorways. And soccer player David Beckham has gone public with his trials with OCD, calling it a "disorder that haunts my life," and asserting that everything in his life has to be in pairs. "I'll put my Pepsi cans in the fridge, and if there's one too many I'll put it in another cupboard," said Beckham, proving that even when acknowledging a mental illness, well-trained athletes can still manage to plug their sponsors.

Clinical Depression

What It Is: Clinical depression is sadness that lasts at least two weeks and is serious enough that it disrupts your social functioning or ability to complete everyday tasks. 16 percent of people experience clinical depression at some point in their lives, but for a smaller segment of the population with major depressive disorders, it's a lifelong struggle.

Geniuses Afflicted: Beginning in his late teens, the brilliant saxophonist Charlie "Bird" Parker dealt with alcoholism, drug addiction, and a crippling depression that led to two suicide attempts. Abraham Lincoln suffered from depression, which he called "the hypo," periodically throughout his adult life. In 1841, Lincoln wrote, "I am now the most miserable man living. Whether I shall ever be better I cannot tell." Charles Darwin also had bouts with depression.

Bipolar Disorder

What It Is: Still sometimes known as manic depression, bipolar disorder is marked by alternating states of depression and mania, an elevated mood with an increase in energy, and a loss of impulse control. While the mania can lead to very strange behavior and psychosis, the greatest risk for suicide comes during periods of bipolar depression.

Geniuses Afflicted: Various psychologists and biographers have retroactively diagnosed hundreds of brilliant minds with manic depression, including Winston Churchill, Ralph Waldo Emerson, Napoléon, Isaac Newton, and Vincent van Gogh. Some of those are likelier candidates than others (it's hard to argue that Van Gogh *wasn't* bipolar, for instance). Jimi Hendrix recorded a song called "Manic Depression," and while it appears he was never diagnosed with the illness, he believed he suffered from it. More recently, child prodigy Dutch Boyd, who graduated from college at 12 and law school at 18 before becoming one of the world's best poker players, was diagnosed with bipolar disorder and institutionalized.

HOW TO DRESS LIKE A POLITICAL GENIUS:

Might as well dye it white now, because you're gonna go gray while in office. In fact, every two-term president since FDR has gotten grayer during their presidential years, and white hair seemed to work pretty well for the first thirteen presidents. (Franklin Pierce was the first brunette.)

Legend has it that just days before he imposed the Cuban embargo, President John F. Kennedy imported 1,000 Cuban cigars. Other democratically elected cigar smokers included Bill Clinton and Winston Churchill.

Blue's probably your best bet. Experts disagree over whether red or blue is the more effective tie-color choice—but outside of St. Patrick's Day, you rarely see a democratically elected leader these days who isn't wearing one of the two. Red supposedly lends color to the face on television, but recent history has favored blue: While John Kerry and Bob Dole prefer red ties, presidents George W. Bush and Bill Clinton both usually wear blue

DEMOCRATICALLY ELECTED

HOW TO DRESS LIKE A POLITICAL GENIUS:

It doesn't have to be the Hussein beret pictured here, but you will need to pick a hat. Pol Pot had the Britney Spears pageboy cap; Mao Zedong often wore a floppy number with a short brim; and of course, if you're going to rule via divine right monarchy, you could always consider a jewel-encrusted crown. They're available in certain castles in Europe, and stateside in most Burger Kings.

If they're good enough for Stalin, Saddam Hussein, and Hitler—then they're good enough for you. But remember: It's not enough to grow a mustache. You have to be really sensitive about it. Hitler tried to kill an adviser who encouraged him to grow his mustache across his entire lip, and Stalin had a poet sent to the gulags for comparing his 'stache to a cockroach.

Amin's general's coat was adorned with dozens of medals, some bigger than a hockey puck. But remember, ix-nay on the edals-may if you're a *communist* dictator; such showy displays of wealth aren't in keeping with your fake empathy for the working class.

DICTATOR

Durable, washable, and flattering to any build, a military uniform reminds your terrified citizens who has the guns: You do! Whether you rose to power as an actual general, like Pakistan's Pervez Musharraf, or you're just a low-level army guy pretending to be a general, like Idi Amin, the uniform lends you a terrifying authenticity you can't get from any power tie.

135

IF IT'S TOO
LATE FOR YOU:
THE MUSICAL EDITION

Want to raise a baby who's a musical prodigy? Throw away that *Baby Mozart* video and follow these proven strategies:

Strategy 1: Practice, Practice, Practice, and When That's Done, Practice More or You Will Be Beaten.

Worked for: **Wolfgang Amadeus Mozart.** Mozart is probably history's most famous child prodigy. He began composing music when he was just 5, and played before the Austrian empress at 6. By 15, he was engaging in the illegal downloading of his day: Mozart attended a performance of a piece that was only allowed to be played in the Sistine Chapel, transcribed the piece after hearing it just once, and thus was responsible for the first pirated copies. Some still argue that Mozart's musical genius was innate, but having one of the world's finest music teachers as a dad who pushed him constantly helped, too: Experts estimate that by the time he was 5, Mozart had endured as many hours composing and playing as the average musically inclined teenagers of his day, which probably accounts for his early success.

Strategy 2: If That Doesn't Work, Learn to Lie.

Worked for: **Cole Porter.** Born and raised amid the bright lights of Peru, Indiana, Cole Porter's mother, Kate, *tried* to raise him in the Mozart manner. He learned violin at 6, piano at 8, and was always pushed to practice more. But Porter just didn't become prodigiously brilliant quickly enough. What to do? The cunning Ms. Porter shaved two years off Cole's age when registering him for music classes, so he'd at least seem advanced. It worked, of course: Porter was just 24 when his first song appeared on Broadway, and today he's remembered as one of America's best songwriters.

Strategy 3: Don't Let Them Have Friends.

Worked for: **Bob Dylan.** Growing up in Minnesota, Robert Zimmerman was a smart, shy kid who spent a lot of time listening to the radio, mainly because he was a bit of a nerd. Although he actually belonged to a *fraternity* during his brief stay at the University of Minnesota, Robert wasn't terribly well-liked there, either. But all it took was a name change and a few hit records, and Bobby quickly became the coolest funky-haired Jewish cat since Al Einstein.

Strategy 4: Get Divorced and Change Continents.

Worked for: Born in New York City, **Maria Callas** (Kalogeropoulos before her father's name change), might never have become the world's foremost soprano (pre-Tony, anyway) had it not been for her parents' divorce when she was a preteen. Maria's mom returned to her native Greece with Maria in tow, and almost immediately enrolled Maria in a conservatory. Just a year later, when Maria was 15, she debuted onstage doing a duet from *Tosca*. By 18, she was a professional.

Strategy 5: If You Want Your Kids to Sing the Blues, Have 'Em Live the Blues.

Worked for: **Ella Fitzgerald.** Her parents' marriage broke up when she was an infant. Then her mother died in a car accident when Ella was 15, and she went to live with her maternal aunt. Ella soon dropped out of school and was sent to a reformatory. She then ran away and spent weeks homeless—all before she was old enough to drive. At 16, Ella stumbled into a little luck, though. She won a drawing and got to sing at one of the first Amateur Nights at the famed Apollo Theater. She brought the house down, and never looked back.

HEISENBERG'S UNCERTAINTY PRINCIPLE

As far as genius stuff goes, the Heisenberg Uncertainty Principle is actually quite easy to understand: It states that you cannot assign exact values for the position *and* the momentum (i.e., the object's mass times the velocity) of an elementary particle like an electron.

Truth be told, the science of measurement has always been inexact, but for centuries, scientists figured that their measurements were wrong because their tools were flawed: A ruler, for instance, isn't terribly reliable when it comes to measuring nanometers. But German physicist Werner Heisenberg proved that even an infinitely accurate measuring tool wouldn't be up to the task. According to the Uncertainty Principle, it is impossible, even in theory, to make an infinitely accurate observation of *both* a particle's position and its momentum. In fact, the more certain a measurement of one becomes, the less certain the measurement of the other becomes.

The Uncertainty Principle has a number of wide-ranging consequences for how we observe the world. One such problem is that if you can't accurately measure both speed and position, it's somewhat difficult to teleport entire human beings

Heisenberg's Uncertain Legacy

Although he disagreed with the Nazis, Heisenberg remained in Germany throughout World War II, and probably worked on Germany's atomic bomb projects. Some have argued that Heisenberg intentionally slowed the progress of Germany's nuclear project, while others say he had no qualms about it whatsoever. In September 1941, he met his old friend Niels Bohr in Copenhagen, and there has long been speculation (as dramatized in the Pulitzer Prize–winning play *Copenhagen*) that Bohr and Heisenberg fought about Germany's attempts to make a bomb. Shortly after the visit, their friendship ended, and Bohr went to America to work on the Manhattan Project.

in a timely fashion to and from a specific place, which is why *Star Trek* features a device known as the Heisenberg Compensator, which by the 24th century will magically make the Uncertainty Principle irrelevant.

But the biggest difficulty with Heisenberg's Uncertainty Principle is the mere idea of it, which one of Heisenberg's physicist contemporaries called "repulsive." For so long, science had been built upon the idea that we were coming closer to a full understanding of the universe, and the Uncertainty Principle holds that at least in some arenas of investigation, full knowledge isn't even theoretically possible. It was in response to these implications of the Uncertainty Principle that Albert Einstein allegedly said, "I cannot accept that God would choose to play dice with the Universe." (Heisenberg's collaborator Niels Bohr responded, "Einstein, don't tell God what to do.") But despite the uproar, and Einstein's disapproval, Heisenberg won the Nobel Prize for Physics in 1932 for his work. The Uncertainty Principle remained Heisenberg's greatest accomplishment. He even joked about it on the inscription he had written on his tombstone: "He lies here, somewhere."

Physics Joke

The next time you're in a roomful of physicists, this one is guaranteed to kill: So a physicist is driving down the highway and gets pulled over. The police officer walks up to the car and asks, "Sir, do you know how fast you were going?" And the physicist answers, "No, but I know *exactly* where I am."

ENOUGH ABOUT YOU: THE GENIUS GUIDE TO CELEBRATING YOUR OWN GENIUS

By and large, geniuses are the first people to recognize the scope of their own brilliance—so it's going to be necessary to put aside your modesty for this journey, just like these folks did.

James Joyce is not world-renowned for his humility. The penultimate line of his semi-autobiographical first novel, *Portrait of the Artist as a Young Man*, after all, is "I go now to forge in the smithy of my soul the uncreated conscience of my race." Even earlier, he showed his high opinion of himself. When the young, still unpublished Joyce had the opportunity to meet the greatest poet Ireland ever produced, W. B. Yeats, Joyce reportedly said, "We have met too late. You are too old for me to have any effect on you." And Joyce didn't mellow with age. In fact, his last words had a condescending ring. Just before dying, Joyce asked, "Does nobody understand?"

There has never been a military genius like *Alexander the Great*, who conquered half the known world in a decade of near-constant warfare. And there has never been an ego quite like his, either. Alexander named no fewer than *nineteen* cities Alexandria and called himself The Divine King to the Asiatics. Alexander declared himself a god and expected to be worshiped as one. But it may be that he was only stating what he literally believed: When he was a child, Alexander's mother reportedly told him again and again that he was a son of Zeus.

Although he could be charming and gracious, nuclear physicist **J. Robert Oppenheimer** was also famously arrogant. In fact, in graduate school, Oppenheimer's classmates signed a petition stating that unless the teacher, Max Born*, agreed to rein in the "child prodigy," they would all quit attending the class. (Among the signatories was future Nobel Prize winner Maria Goppert.) Oppenheimer didn't do himself any favors when he eschewed all modesty in the moments after the first atomic bomb was successfully tested in New Mexico. Quoting the *Bhagavad-Gita*, Oppenheimer announced, "Now, I am become Death [Shiva], the destroyer of worlds."

A lot of people loved **Salvador Dalí** for his charming eccentricity, but nobody—and we mean nobody—loved him quite as much as he loved himself. "Every morning upon awakening," Dalí once said, "the I experience a supreme pleasure: that of being Salvador Dalí." Dalí's surrealistic, dreamlike, symbol-heavy paintings shook up the art world, but Dalí's image was nearly as important as his work. While other Spanish surrealists like Joan Miró became famous in the art world, Dalí's celebrity transcended his paintings. He appeared on the television game show "What's My Line?", for instance, and wrote the dream sequence in the 1945 Alfred Hitchcock film *Spellbound*.

Ayn Rand fancied herself the philosophical equal of Aristotle and Thomas Aquinas, but egotism was all part of her philosophy. Famous for her weighty novels *Atlas Shrugged* and *The Fountainhead*, which high-school students have been lugging

---

* Totally off-topic, but Max Born, who won the Nobel Prize for Physics in 1954, was the maternal grandfather of major genius and *Grease* star Olivia Newton-John.

A Little Humility

Of course, not all geniuses are relentless egotists. Occasionally, you'll meet a meek and modest person who doesn't need self-promotion to push himself along. Such was the case with Leonardo da Vinci. Despite being a brilliant painter, engineer, inventor, sculptor, and costar of the magnificent Drew Barrymore vehicle *Ever After*, Leonardo was always humble when appraising his own work. In fact, it's said that his last words were, "I have offended God and man because my work wasn't good enough." Would that you could take a scoop of that and sprinkle it on Tom Cruise, Leo.

around for decades, Rand's objectivism championed ego and condemned all forms of altruism, on account of how helping the weak only slows progress. All of Rand's protagonists resembled the way she saw herself: initially shunned because of their brilliance, they eventually emerge triumphant. Well, maybe not so triumphant: None of Rand's books made the Modern Library's critics' list of the Top 100 books of the 20th century.

IF YA GOTTA GO: DYING LIKE A GENIUS (LAST WORDS)

Unless you or one of your fellow geniuses manages to invent a living-forever machine (the technical term), you're probably going to die. But that doesn't mean you can't bow out of this world in a manner truly befitting a genius. To do that, you'll need to make sure you have some great last words. For inspiration, just bone up with some of the greats:

Dying in a garishly decorated hotel room, Irish playwright **Oscar Wilde** summoned his last measure of strength to say, "My wallpaper and I are fighting a duel to the death. One or other of us has got to go." In doing so, the often-hilarious Wilde established the high bar for humorous last words.

Speaking of funny Irish playwrights: **Brendan Behan** (author of *The Quare Fellow*, among others), died in a Catholic hospital. His last words were spoken to a nun taking his vital signs. "Bless you, Sister," Behan said. "May all your sons be bishops."

At least two geniuses have mentioned champagne on their way out. Short story writer **Anton Chekhov** (d. 1904) said, "It's been a long time since I had champagne." The British economist **John Maynard Keynes** (d. 1946) felt similarly wistful, noting, "I should have drunk more champagne."

Q. What did children's author **Hans Christian Andersen** and pianist **Frédéric Chopin** have in common? A. They were both geniuses, and they were both terrified of being buried alive (known as taphephobia). Dying of tuberculosis, Chopin's last words were, "Swear to make them cut me open so I won't be buried alive."

The short story writer **O. Henry** had the kind of fantastic ending for which his stories were famous. "Turn up the lights," he announced. "I don't want to go home in the dark."

On August 16, 1977, **Elvis Presley** showed the kind of class and sophistication that marked the final years of his life when he announced to his girlfriend, "I'm going to the can, Ginger."

Asked if he had any parting words of advice, the morbidly ill hotelier **Conrad Hilton** (d. 1979) told his children, "Leave the shower curtain on the inside of the tub." (He might have added, "Oh, and if you happen to have a kid named Paris two years from now, keep her locked inside the house forever and ever.")

Pancho Villa was a brilliant, if ruthless, general. But when he was assassinated in 1923, he proved to be something less than a genius: "Don't let it end like this," Villa said in parting. "Tell them I said something."

The Greek mathematician **Archimedes** (d. 212 BCE) was sketching an equation in the sand when a Roman soldier charged up and began to walk over Archimedes's work. "Don't disturb my equation," Archimedes said, whereupon he was promptly killed.

Peter Pan creator **J. M. Barrie** (d. 1937) said, "I can't sleep." Sure you can, Mr. Barrie. And soundly.

Casanova, famous for his thoroughly amoral sexual exploits, devoted his last words to hedging his bets. "I have lived as a philosopher, and die as a Christian."

When the dying German composer **Christoph Gluck** (d. 1787) was asked whether the role of Christ in *The Last Judgment* should be played by a tenor or a bass, Gluck responded, "If you wait a little, I shall be able to tell you from personal experience."

For whatever reason, the real geniuses among Confederate generals in the American Civil War tended to have beautiful last words. After being shot by his own men, **Stonewall Jackson** famously said, "Let us cross over the river and rest under the shade of those trees" (although his actual last words, "I have always wished to die on a Sunday," were spoken a couple days later). Decades after the war, **Robert E. Lee**'s final declaration called to mind his days on the battlefield: "Strike the tent!"

Of course, one general from the Union's side had an eloquent statement of his own. On his deathbed, a fading **Ulysses S. Grant** passed notes to his doctors about his condition and the effectiveness of their various treatments. And while his actual last words seem to have been a request for water, the last thing he penned was quite beautiful (at least to anyone who likes grammar), "The fact is I think I am a verb instead of a personal pronoun. A verb is anything that signifies to be; to do; or to suffer. I signify all three."

Benjamin Franklin's last words revealed his cranky underbelly. When asked to roll over so that he could breathe easier, an exasperated Franklin replied, "A dying man can do nothing easy." It's hard to make a case that veteran Hollywood actor **Edmund Gwenn** was a *genius*, but his last words are relevant here next to Franklin's. When someone said "This must be very hard for you," Gwenn responded, "Yes, it's tough—but it's not as tough as doing comedy."

The Welsh poet **Dylan Thomas**'s last words are generally recorded as "I've had eighteen straight whiskeys. I believe that's the record." He *did* say that, and those 18 whiskeys did directly lead to his death, but his *last* words were the more likely, "After 39 years, this is all I've done."

When Enlightenment philosopher **Voltaire** was asked on his deathbed to renounce Satan, Voltaire wryly responded, "Now now, dear Sir, this is not the time to be making enemies."

As bitter good-byes go, no one can match the poet **Sara Teasdale** (1884–1933), whose poetic suicide note was written to a lover who'd spurned her:

> "When I am dead, and over me bright April
> Shakes out her rain drenched hair,
> Tho you should lean above me broken-hearted,
> I shall not care.
> For I shall have peace
> As leafy trees are peaceful
> When rain bends down the bough.
> And I shall be more silent and cold-hearted
> Than you are now."

After his wife told him, "Good night," steel tycoon **Andrew Carnegie** responded, "I hope so." He died before morning.

During his final illness, the inventor **Thomas Edison** (d. 1931) was looking out over his Menlo Park home and laboratory—and perhaps staring farther afield than that—when he wistfully remarked to his wife, "It's very beautiful over there."

Ludwig van Beethoven's last words are recorded variously as "Friends, applaud, the comedy is over," "I shall hear in heaven," or "Too bad! It's too late!" All three of which seem rather eloquent for a guy who was dying a miserable death—probably from lead poisoning.

80%

genius

Congratulations! You are now 80% of the way toward full-fledged Genius.

At this point, you remind us a little of Rosalind Franklin (1920–1958), the scientist whose research into X-ray crystallography proved absolutely critical to James Watson and Francis Crick's uncovering the structure of DNA. Doubtless, Franklin was a genius. She overcame discrimination against women, which was pervasive in science, to become one of the most promising young chemists in the world. Many even argue that she deserved a share of the Nobel Prize Watson and Crick won. But Franklin never quite grasped the double helical shape of DNA before Watson and Crick published their results. You've come a long, long way—but to ensure that you don't end up under-heralded and shafted of all that Nobel Prize money, press on!

SPILLING THE DIRT ON SOME BRILLIANT CLASSICAL COMPOSERS

The Man: Johann Sebastian Bach (1685–1750)

The Music: Everything from organ works to cello suites. The greatest of the Baroque composers, Bach is famous for his dense melodies, which through counterpoint—the playing of several musical lines simultaneously—were heightened, transformed, and sometimes inverted as a piece progressed.

The Dirt: By the time Johann came along, Bach's family had already produced so many famous composers and musicians that *Bach* had become a German word for *musician*. Bach himself spawned plenty of Bachs. He had a total of 20 children; 7 from his marriage to his cousin, Maria Barbara Bach, and 13 with his second wife, Anna Magdalena Walken.

The Man: George Frideric Handel (1685–1759)

The Music: Handel's most famous piece is undoubtedly the *Messiah*, an oratorio that sets text from the King James Bible to gorgeously polyphonic music. Handel supposedly wept while writing it, overcome by how beautiful it was. (We can just picture it: "I am such a genius! *Sob.* Ah, what a pleasure to see these beautiful notes spring forth from my pen! *Sob.*")

The Dirt: Although it's got a lofty title and religious themes, Handel composed the *Messiah* for the most secular of reasons: He was out of money. Looking for a quick buck, Handel composed the *Messiah* in just 24 days during the summer of 1741.

The Man: Wolfgang Amadeus Mozart (1756–1791)

The Music: A versatile composer who wrote everything from operas to symphonies to piano sonatas to popular dances, Mozart's work was marked by clarity and delicacy. Undoubtedly, the master of the classical style, his compositions are by and large some of the least depressing in all of classical music.

The Dirt: Mozart was kind of a perv. You think Snoop Dogg has a flair for the obscene? Well, for a party, Mozart once wrote a canon to the lyric, "Lick my [explicit location deleted out of a sense of common decency] nice and clean." Who's down with O.P.P.? Wolfgang Amadeus, apparently.

The Man: Ludwig van Beethoven (1770–1827)

The Music: The brilliant composer who created some of his most lasting works after losing his hearing, Beethoven's nine symphonies (the last of which features the famous "Ode to Joy," which we find almost as hard to get out of our heads as Tom Petty's "Free Fallin'*") bridge the gap between the classical and romantic eras in music.

The Dirt: Well, Beethoven himself was not dirty. In fact, he washed himself compulsively. But his *clothes* were very dirty, indeed. Although he was never poor, Beethoven often walked the streets of Vienna wearing stinking, filthy rags and muttering to

---

* For more on this phenomenon, see p. 183.

himself. Such eccentric behavior may have been caused by the lead poisoning that probably killed him.

The Man: Robert Schumann (1810–1856)

The Music: One of the great Romantic composers, Schumann had periods of extraordinary productivity—in one year, he wrote 168 songs. His compositions feature complex harmonies and a whimsy not seen in the Classical composers who came before him.

The Dirt: Schumann was crippled by mental illness in the last 20 years of his life. He feared metal, attempted suicide, and constantly heard the note A playing inside his head. Well, better the the note A than "Oh Mickey, you're so fine." Man, we've had that song in our heads for like a decade and we haven't composed a thing.

The Man: Richard Wagner (1813–1883)

The Music: German opera buff Wagner was about more than just music—his essays on musical theory were hugely influential—but he's most famous for the densely orchestrated operas such as *Tristan and Isolde* and *The Valkyrie*. Wagner is also notable for his deft use of leitmotifs, melodic themes that connect the music to characters or plotlines.

The Dirt: The biggest skeleton in Wagner's closet is doubtlessly his rabid anti-Semitism, which may have been due in part to his rivalry with Jewish composers like Felix Mendelssohn. Wagner called Jewish people "freaks of nature," and he advocated the eradication of Judaism, if not—as the Nazis later argued—the elimination of Jews themselves.

The Woman: Clara Schumann (1819–1896)

The Music: One of the greatest pianists of her generation, Clara also composed quite a lot of major works for piano, all while raising seven children with her husband, the aforementioned Robert Schumann.

The Dirt: Clara's self-doubt, combined with her duties as a wife and mother, hindered her productivity. At 20, she wrote, "I once believed I possessed creative talent, but I have given up this idea; a woman must not desire to compose." She is nonetheless remembered as one of the greatest female composers of the 19th century. She's so widely admired, in fact, that she appears on the back of the German 100 Deutsche Mark bill.

The Man: Peter Ilych Tchaikovsky (1840–1893)

The Music: Tchaikovsky utilized music from Western Europe along with folk melodies from his native Russia to create allur-ingly rich harmonic piano concertos and ballets (*Swan Lake*, *The Nutcracker*), as well operas like *Eugene Onegin*.

The Dirt: Tchaikovsky, who is universally acknowledged to have been homosexual, experienced what has to be the short-est 24-year marriage ever: After marrying a woman he barely knew, Tchaikovsky regretted the decision so deeply that within two weeks, he attempted suicide. A month later, he abandoned his wife forever, whereupon she went insane and ended up in a sanitarium. Tchaikovsky never saw her again, but they remained legally married until her death 24 years later.

The Man: Arnold Schoenberg (1874–1951)

The Music: One of the first composers to abandon traditional tonality, Schoenberg invented the "twelve-tone technique," which was later used by the likes of Igor Stravinsky and Pierre

GENIUS INSTRUCTION MANUAL

Boulez, even though to most people twelve-tone compositions do not sound—uh, how do we put this—good.

The Dirt: Schoenberg suffered from triskaidekaphobia, fear of the number 13. He took an *a* out of Aaron's name in his opera *Moses and Aron* so the title wouldn't have 13 letters. Schoenberg, as it turns out, had reason to be scared: He died on Friday, the 13th of June, 1951. He was 76 years old (add up those digits).

The Man: Igor Stravinsky (1882–1971)

The Music: Among the greatest modern classical composers, Stravinsky wrote everything from symphonies to cantatas. But his most beloved works are the revolutionary dissonant ballets *The Rite of Spring* and *The Firebird*.

The Dirt: Many in the relatively staid world of classical music weren't ready for Stravinsky's modernism. In 1923, one newspaper called his work a "nightmare of noise and eccentricity," and the audience at the 1913 premiere of *The Rite of Spring* found the ballet so repulsive they literally rioted. (Stravinsky claimed not to be bothered by such responses. In fact, he once said his goal was to take his audience and, through his music, send "them all to hell.")

HOW TO LOVE LIKE
A GENIUS

Of course, there are a lot of geniuses in human history, and it's dangerous to make broad assumptions about how brilliant individuals structure their love lives. That said, an awful lot of geniuses try the same two Romantic Strategies:

Strategy 1: MARRY YOUR COUSIN

Employed by: Charles Darwin, Albert Einstein, Edgar Allan Poe, and Lewis Carroll.

The Risks: Most studies indicate that cousin marriage slightly (but only slightly) increases the risk of recessive genetic diseases, such as cystic fibrosis, in offspring, from about 5 percent to about 7 percent. The other risk, of course, is that it's gross. Also, it's illegal in 20 states—including Mississippi *and* West Virginia, so enough with the jokes already.

The Rewards: Well, it worked out pretty well for a lot of the geniuses mentioned above. Darwin and his wife had a profoundly happy marriage (and 10 children), tainted only by Darwin's lack of Christian faith. Einstein had a miserable first marriage until he ditched that wife for his cousin Elsa, to whom he remained married for decades. And while both Poe and Carroll were a little fixated on teenagers (Poe married his cousin when she was just 13), both marriages lasted a lifetime.

Although, Then Again: You'll note that while a lot of geniuses *engaged* in cousin love, we don't have a long list of geniuses who were the *offspring* of cousin love.

Anecdotally: To compound the ick factor, Poe called his cousin-bride "Sis."

Strategy 2: LOVE THY WIFE'S SISTER

Employed by: Charles Dickens, Sigmund Freud, Wolfgang Mozart, and Peter Paul Rubens.

The Risks: It doesn't really bode well for your marriage. Take Dickens. It is said that Dickens was in love with *two* of his wife's sisters—Mary, who died in 1837, and then Georgina. But even two sisters and one wife (who bore him 10 children, so they couldn't have been *that* unhappy) wasn't enough for Dickens: He had a decades-long affair with an actress named Ellen Ternan. The infidelities cost him his marriage (although even after Dickens' wife left him, her sister Georgina continued to live with him).

The Rewards: Well, the rewards are pretty obvious, really—but beloved sisters-in-law also make for great muses. For Mozart, his love for sister-in-law Aloysia was at least partly because of her voice—he wrote some of his best choral music for her. For Rubens, his (Rubenesque, needless to say) sister-in-law served as the naked model for some of his most erotic paintings. In short, it was all about *fueling the genius*. Oh, and also the sex.

Although, Then Again: In most of these cases, there's no hard evidence that there ever even was sex—just unrequited love.

You'd think that geniuses would generally be pretty desirable, but somehow or another they always manage to find some unrequited love.

Anecdotally: Freud's affair (if it ever happened) with his sister-in-law was an important facet of his break with Carl Jung, who early in his career played Robin to Freud's Batman. Jung claimed Freud's sister-in-law confessed the affair to him. The revelation, he wrote, caused him "agony"— a pretty self-righteous reaction considering Jung had had at least two extramarital affairs of his own.

The Legality of Cousin Love

Marriage between first cousins is legal (as of 2006) in the following states: Alabama, Alaska, Arizona*, California, Colorado, Connecticut, Florida, Georgia, Hawaii, Illinois*, Indiana*, Maine*, Maryland, Massachusetts, New Jersey, New Mexico, New York, North Carolina, Rhode Island, South Carolina, Tennessee, Texas, Utah*, Vermont, Virginia and Wisconsin*.

(* Only if you can prove to a court that you're incapable of bearing offspring.)

Some Other Romantic Strategies:

Strategy 3: MARRIAGE ISN'T FOREVER, BUT NEITHER IS DIVORCE

Geniuses can be fiery, impulsive people. So it's no surprise that they periodically end a relationship only to realize— hey—maybe this could work after all. The habitually unfaithful Dorothy Parker divorced her husband Alan Campbell in 1949 only to remarry him a few years later (although she never stopped cheating). And the playwright Neil "Brighton Beach Memoirs" Simon divorced his wife Diane Lander in 1988, remarried her in 1990, and then divorced her again.

But now and again there's a genuinely inspiring reason to pull the ole unmarry-remarry. Russian novelist Alexander Solzhenitsyn, who spent time in a prison camp during Stalin's reign in the USSR, divorced his wife Natalia to protect her from persecution. He remarried her a few years after Stalin's death. Heartening story, but the postscript takes the bloom off the rose: Solzhenitsyn and Natalia divorced again in 1972, not because of political pressure, but because Solzhenitsyn wanted to marry someone else.

Strategy 4: THE BEST LOVE IS NO LOVE AT ALL

Playwright and Nobel laureate George Bernard Shaw, who coined the phrase "Youth is wasted on the young," made sure his virginity was not wasted on his youth: He lost it at the ripe age of 29, to a widow 15 years his senior. Apparently, it wasn't all that good though, because most scholars believe Shaw rarely, if ever, had intimate physical relationships thereafter—not even with his wife, to whom he was married for 45 years.

Prominent scientists who never married and may well have died virgins: Isaac Newton, Nikola Tesla, and John Harvey Kellogg.

Speaking of Kellogg, who invented the corn flake: He was married more than 40 years. But all seven of their children were adopted, and Kellogg was a vociferous anti-sex advocate, who claimed never to engage in it with others—or even with himself. To alleviate what he called "self-abuse" (that is, masturbation), Kellogg recommended boys be circumcised "by a surgeon without administering an anesthetic." As for girls, Kellogg wrote, "the author has found the application of pure carbolic acid to the clitoris an excellent means of allaying abnormal excitement." No wonder his poor wife steered clear of him.

Strategy 5: CHEAT RELENTLESSLY

Comic actor, playwright, and screenwriter W. C. Fields's last words were, "God damn the whole friggin' world and everyone in it but you, Carlotta," which sounds very romantic until you consider that his (estranged) wife was named Hattie. Carlotta was his mistress.

Lord Byron, the Wilt Chamberlain of his day, slept with an awful lot of women. Now, we're not here to judge, but many have speculated that one of Byron's paramours was none other than his half sister Augusta Leigh, who at the time was—besides being his *sister*—married. Some scholars believe, in fact, that Augusta's daughter, Medora, was Byron's—making Medora both his niece and his daughter.

OPEN-HEART SURGERY IN 7 EASY STEPS

Note: Never, ever, ever use this guide to perform open-heart surgery. Just use it to make your friends *think* you can perform open heart surgery. Okay, moving on:

Step 1. Make an incision through the breastbone, retract the patient's rib cage so as to expose the heart, and cut open the heart's lining, known as the pericardium. Oh, wait a second.

Step 2. Belatedly put your very annoyed patient under general anesthesia.

Step 3. *Now* do all that other stuff. Okay, time to stop the heart. Place the plastic tubes of your heart-lung bypass machine (if you've gotten this far and have forgotten to bring along your heart-lung bypass machine, we are in a world of trouble) into the heart's right atrium. These tubes will suck impure blood into the machine, which will oxygenate it and return it to the body via the tube going into the aorta, which you also need to insert.

Step 4. Cool the heart with a potassium solution, which will slowly—and hopefully safely—stop the patient's heart. If you'd rather not merely cool the heart, some recent research suggests that you might get away with cooling the entire patient's body—it's experimental, but hey, what do you have to lose? Oh, right. The patient.

Step 5. At this point, you need to fix whatever's wrong with the heart, and don't dawdle, because these heart-lung bypass machines don't work forever. Say there's a hole between chambers in the heart. You'll need to sew a patch into the tiny hole. Make sure your stitches are secure—they'll hopefully last decades. If you're dealing with a bypass surgery, you'll need to sew a vein from the patient's leg (you didn't get a leg vein earlier? Jeez—okay, grab it now, but hurry) around the arterial blockage, so that the vein can serve as a bypass (get it?) for blood trying to make its way through the body. If you're looking at a quadruple or quintuple bypass, settle in, because you'll be at this for a while.

Step 6. Re-close the heart's lining and it's time to heat that thumper back up, baby. A defibrillator should do the trick now—just a little electric kick, and *bam*, it's back. Once you're confident the heart is beating normally, you can slowly increase the amount of work the heart is doing and decrease the work of the heart-lung bypass machine, until finally it's time to remove the machine altogether.

Step 7. Now you just need to close up the ribcage and sew the patient's chest back together, and accept congratulations from your friends, colleagues, and eventually your patient, provided s/he survived.

STRING THEORY

For almost a century, theoretical physicists from Albert Einstein to Stephen Hawking have been searching for the elusive "unified field theory," a single elegant theorem that can account for the movement and force behind all matter in the universe. Einstein never achieved his goal. But these days, it seems more and more possible that a theorem that could fit on a bumper sticker might explain the behavior of all matter. (Well, no theorem will ever explain the behavior of Geraldo Rivera. By "all matter," scientists mostly mean stuff that doesn't talk, on which—as you may have noticed—they tend to be rather fixated.

The goal of a unified field theory is to unify the four fields, or forces, of nature:

Field 1: Strong force. This sounds like it was made up by the screenwriter of *Superman 3* or something, but strong force is the glue that holds quarks together to form neutrons and protons, and that holds neutrons and protons together to form nuclei. (To achieve a nuclear reaction, you have to overcome strong force, which is thankfully difficult, or else there would be constant nuclear explosions occurring throughout the universe!)

Field 2: Electromagnetic force. Remember the Empire's tractor beam that captured Han Solo's Millennium Falcon? Electromagnetic force at work. (More commonly, it's also seen affecting electrically charged particles.)

Field 3: "Weak force" sounds puny, but isn't. While it has a short range, weak force is responsible for radioactivity, which can be quite bad for you.

Field 4: Gravitational force, or the reason that apples fall in orchards, and the moon orbits the earth.

Those who believe in a Theory of Everything assert that all four forces are mere manifestations of the same natural law. But for decades, little progress was made toward *finding* that law. Then, along came string theory. In 1970, three physicists proposed that the fundamental building block of matter was not pointed particles, as had long been suspected, but rather tiny, vibrating, 1-dimensional loops of string. These loops of string are approximately 10^{-35} meters in length, which means that if you were to magnify a hydrogen atom to the point where it was as big as the solar system, the strings inside the atom would be about the size of Andre the Giant. Needless to say, we cannot see them.

But the presence of these strings explains a lot. For example, one of the big problems of contemporary physics is that, at least as they are currently understood, the theories of quantum mechanics and general relativity cannot both be right. The reasons for this are pretty complex, but at any rate it has had physicists in a tizzy for a long time. In the 1980s, however, physicists realized that the different vibrations of the subatomic strings could account for this discrepancy. String theorists often use a musical metaphor: A violin string vibrates to make music, and as any parent of a third-grade violinist knows, a single string can

What the Strings Look Like

It is, admittedly, somewhat difficult to imagine a 1-dimensional object floating in space. In his book *The Elegant Universe*, Brian Greene describes the strings as "infinitely thin rubber bands." And they are literally *infinitely* thin, because for string theory to make sense, the strings must exist in only one dimension; i.e., they can have length but no width. How is this possible? Mathematically, the concept relies partly on an understanding of the infinitesimal given to us by none other than Georg Cantor, whom you no doubt remember vividly from p. 45. It all folds back upon itself, this genius stuff.

make a huge variety of sounds depending on its vibration. So, too, with the vibrations of subatomic strings. According to string theory, a kind of massive symphony underlies the universe.

That's an elegant image, and it explains a lot. For instance, it could well be the underlying principle behind the aforementioned "four forces." The four forces may just represent different notes the strings can play, or different ways in which they can vibrate. But as promising as it seems, the evidence for string theory is still circumstantial, and the strings will never be viewable unless a microscope comes along that is exponentially more powerful than anything we can even imagine today.

Still, string theory may well be one of the final steps on the road toward a Theory of Everything. Really, all we need now is a more complete understanding of the how and why of the strings' vibrations. You should start researching that, actually, just as soon as you finish this book.

90%

genius

Congratulations! You are now 90% of the way toward full-fledged Genius.

Oh, you're close. So very, very close. On the genius scale, you are now entering Stephen Hawking territory: You're famous, well-respected by the public and your scientific peers, and unquestionably brilliant. Now if you could just figure out a universal field theory (aka a Theory of Everything). Hawking, who holds the position at Cambridge University once occupied by none other than Isaac Newton, has made significant contributions to many branches of theoretical physics, including string theory. He has also published compelling mathematical evidence that the universe began with a Big Bang. But that universal field theory, the holy grail of physics, has eluded him just as it did Einstein before him. Perhaps Einstein and Hawking both have left it to you to figure out. Well, okay. Probably not. But you're still nearly a Certified* Genius.

---

*   Note: Certification process is not accredited, and come to think of it, does not technically exist. But if these last few pages don't get you into Mensa—jeez, we don't know what to tell you.

SOME PITFALLS YOU'LL REALLY NEED TO AVOID

As you inch closer to full-blown geniusity, you should keep in mind that genius has both its risks and its rewards. You will need to assiduously avoid some of the more tragic fates that often befall the genius, including these:

Pitfall 1: ALWAYS FALLING FOR THE WRONG PEOPLE

We're not dissing unrequited love. Without his Beatrice, after all, Dante might never have been inspired to write great poetry. Just don't get taken on a ride you'll regret. Renaissance sculptor Michelangelo fell in love with several young men, including a few who posed for him, but almost every one of them proved to be a scoundrel: One lover stole his money flat-out; another, the hilariously named Febbo di Poggio, asked for money immediately after Michelangelo recited a florid love poem he'd written for young Febbo di Poggio. Didn't Febbo care at all how hard it is to find words that rhyme with Poggio?!

Not until he was 57 did Michelangelo finally meet Tomasso dei Cavalieri, a guy who stole his heart but not his wallet: He remained devoted to Cavalieri for decades, although some scholars argue their love remained forever platonic.

Pitfall 2: GETTING KNIFED IN A BAR FIGHT

If you don't believe this is worth worrying about, just ask basketball star—genius might be pushing it—Paul Pierce, who nearly died after being stabbed several times in a nightclub in 2000. Or ask the great 16th-century playwright Christopher Marlowe, who was reportedly stabbed to death in a bar brawl way back in 1593. Well, you can't ask him, because he died. *Or did he?* One of the more out-there theories of Shakespearean authorship is that Marlowe faked his death in the bar fight to deceive his enemies and then returned to playwriting as the incomparable William Shakespeare. If true, faking his death improved the quality of Marlowe's writing exponentially.

Pitfall 3: GOING OFF TO WAR TO GAIN VALUABLE LIFE EXPERIENCE

Now and then, this works pretty well. Geniuses from Kurt Vonnegut (who was a P.O.W. in World War II) to Aeschylus (who fought in the Battle of Marathon) to Dr. Ruth (who was a sniper in the Israeli Army during the 1948 Arab Israeli war) have grown as men and women as a result of their war experiences. But the downside of war is the part about how it can kill you: English poet Wilfred Owen was a well-respected 25-year-old when he was gunned down a month before the end of World War I. The Great War also took the life of the immensely promising young physicist Henry Moseley, who before his 30th birthday explained to the world the importance of the atomic number. After Moseley's death, in fact, the British government ceased allowing prominent scientists to enlist.

Pitfall 4: GOING BALD

This is non-ideal for several reasons—not the least of which is that bald geniuses tend to fare poorly. Look at the evidence: Salman Rushdie ran afoul of the ayatollah; the inarguably brilliant Telly Savalas was divorced twice; Jackson Pollock was an alcoholic; Andre Agassi used to have a mullet; William Burroughs was a heroin addict who shot his wife in the head; Gandhi got assassinated—the list goes on and on. But by far the most disgraceful fate ever to befall a bald man came in Ancient Greece, back when legend and fact co-existed comfortably. Supposedly, the bald playwright Aeschylus died after a vulture dropped a tortoise on his bald head, which the vulture had mistaken for a rock.

Pitfall 5: SWALLOWING SOMETHING OTHER THAN FOOD

This seems like your basic, straightforward advice—not the kind of problem a genius would have to face. And yet historically, "swallowing non-food items" has been a fatal flaw of at least two geniuses. In 1983, the Pulitzer Prize–winning playwright Tennessee Williams choked to death on a the cap of a pill bottle—which sounds like a pretty ridiculous way to die until you compare it to the death of Sherwood Anderson 52 years earlier. Anderson, author of *Winesburg, Ohio,* died of peritonitis after swallowing a toothpick in Panama.

THE HUMAN GENOME PROJECT

Let's begin with a quick refresher course in the world of genes: Genes are slacks, generally blue, made out of denim. The first genes with copper rivets were patented by San Franciscan Levi Strauss in 1872. Oh, wait. Right.

Okay, bear with us here, because it gets really interesting: Genes are the pieces of DNA that are transcribed by cells—first into RNA, and then into proteins. Often called the "building blocks of life," genes contain all that we inherit. DNA—or deoxyribonucleic acid to geniuses—is the double helix–shaped nucleic acid that includes genes, and also includes a lot of other stuff. Each strand of DNA is made up by strings of nucleotides, and there are four such nucleotides: adenine (A), cytosine (C), guanine (G), and thymine (T). Of course, these nucleotides just don't pair off randomly. Instead, each nucleotide base is extremely picky about who it hangs out with: A and T always pair together across strands; same with C and G. Now here's where it starts to get fascinating: These couplings are known as "base pairs," and in its 23 chromosomes, the human genome has about 3 *billion* base pairs.

That's a lot—which accounts for the fact that for several decades after Watson and Crick's discovery of DNA in 1953, no one had attempted to unlock the human genome's secrets nucleotide by nucleotide. But then in 1986, a US Department of Energy employee named Charles DeLisi proposed the Human Genome Project. It began with much fanfare in 1990, with some researchers estimating that the Project might find as many as 2,000,000 genes in humans.

Actually, the *Human* Genome Project is a bit of a misnomer, since the project also sequenced the genes of some of science's favorite animals: the nematode worm (in 1996), *e. coli* (in 1997), the fruit fly (in 2000), and the lab mouse (in 2001), among others. In 2003, the project announced its greatest achievement, though: The entire human genome had been sequenced, with 99.99% accuracy. The results were quite surprising: Human beings don't have 2,000,000 genes; we have fewer than 30,000. The vast majority of DNA, sometimes called "junk DNA," doesn't encode for proteins at all—it just sits there, and no one knows exactly why. (This, incidentally, would be an excellent riddle for you to solve.) Some speculate that junk DNA is necessary for the structure of the molecules;

Clones

You might be thinking, "This is all well and good, but what if I want to create a clone army?" Even with the huge advances made in the field of human genetics, clone armies are imaginable only in the distant future—or a long time ago in a galaxy far, far away. Although the Raelians, a suspicious religious cult whose central beliefs center on knowledge gleaned from aliens, claim to have cloned humans, no one takes them seriously. Of course, even if you could create a clone army, they might not be a very good army. Clones seem to have a lot of health problems, and may age faster than normal organisms: Famed clone Dolly the sheep, for instance, got arthritis when she was just 2.

some think it's leftovers from our pre-human evolutionary past.

Thanks to the Human Genome Project, many scientists now believe that it's not only genes that are important, but also the *regulation* of those genes. The ability to turn protein encoding on and off adds a layer of complexity to the process, and might therefore account for why we are such complicated animals with so few genes. Certainly, the number of genes isn't directly related to the complexity of an organism. Fruit flies, for instance, have only 13,601 genes, while the far simpler roundworm has some 18,000. Since we're talking here about an animal that literally does not know its face from its tuchus, it's hard to imagine that the roundworm is anywhere near as intricate as we are.

SPELLING FOR GENIUSES: 9 WORDS THAT HAVE DECIDED THE NATIONAL SPELLING BEE

1926: ABROGATE

Definition? A verb, meaning to formally abolish.

Language of origin? Latin.

Can you use it in a sentence, please? "Although it had been on life support for some time, disco was truly abrogated on July 12, 1979, at Comiskey Park in Chicago, when 'Disco Demolition Night' led to a riot."

1932: KNACK

Definition? A noun, meaning a specific talent, especially a difficult-to-learn one.

Language of origin? From the Middle English *knakke*.

Can you use it in a sentence, please? "Obviously, you didn't need much of a knack for spelling to win the National Spelling Bee back in 1932."

1951: INSOUCIANT

Definition? An adjective, meaning nonchalant.

Language of origin? French, from Old French and before that from Old Latin.

Can you use it in a sentence, please? "I'm not saying 'whatever' in the passive-aggressive way; I'm saying it in the genuinely insouciant way."

1961: SMARAGDINE

Definition? An adjective, meaning relating to emeralds or colored like emeralds.

Language of origin? Middle English, from Latin and Greek.

Can you use it in a sentence, please? "After riding the tilt-a-whirl, Wilbur took on a bit of a smaragdine hue."

1967: CHIHUAHUA

Definition? Oh, you know what a Chihuahua is.

Language of origin? Named after the state in northern Mexico.

Can you use it in a sentence, please? "At first I thought there was an infestation in her apartment, and then I realized it was just her Chihuahuas."

1987: ODONTALGIA

Definition? A noun, meaning toothache.

Language of origin? Latin.

Can you use it in a sentence, please? "No, I can't use it in a sentence, because this odontalgia hurts so bad I can barely even move my mouth right now."

1994: ANTEDILUVIAN

Definition? An adjective, literally meaning "before the flood" (as in Noah's), this is used to describe anything extremely antiquated.

Language of origin? Latin.

Can you use it in a sentence, please? "Since the advent of spell check and everything, spelling bees might seem a little antediluvian, but then occasionally you will go and use a legitimate word that spell check insists is not a word, such as, say, *vivisepulture.*"

1996: VIVISEPULTURE

Definition? A noun, meaning the act of burying someone or something alive.

Language of origin? Latin.

Can you use it in a sentence, please? "Hans Christian Andersen was so afraid of vivisepulture that every night he put a note by his bedside asserting, 'I only *appear* to be dead.'*"

---

* True story.

10

2003: POCOCURANTE

Definition? An adjective, meaning apathetic, or a noun, meaning one who is apathetic.

Language of origin? Italian, with a Latin root.

Can you use it in a sentence, please? "I'm sorry, but 'pococurante,' as a word, has way too much verve and energy to mean *apathetic*."

YOUR MODEL
LITERARY GENIUS:
MARK TWAIN

Mark Twain (1835–1910) was brash, hilarious, brilliant, best-selling, and quintessentially American. But the real reason we've selected him as your model literary genius is that unlike the vast majority of major writers, Twain had a long and happy marriage. And we here at **mental_floss** want you to be a well-contented genius.

Samuel Clemens grew up in Hannibal, Missouri, a small town on the Mississippi that would be the basis for many of his future novels, including the brilliant *Adventures of Huckleberry Finn* and the relentlessly mediocre *Adventures of Tom Sawyer*. As a young man, Clemens worked as a steamboat captain on the Mississippi (memorably recounted in *Life on the Mississippi*), spent a few hilariously inept weeks with a Confederate militia (recorded in "The Private History of a Campaign That Failed"), and toiled in a Nevada silver mine before turning to newspaper reporting. He soon took on a pseudonym, and as Mark Twain, Clemens began to display his keen wit and great ear for dialogue. In 1867, Twain became a star with his short story, "The Jumping Frog of Calaveras County." Just two years later, his first book, *The Innocents Abroad*, was published. In it, Twain painted himself as an unpretentious everyman—"They spell it

Vinci and pronounce it Vinchy; foreigners always spell better than they pronounce," he wrote. But the Western everyman soon abandoned his old life for the wealth of the Northeast, where he lived the rest of his years.

He married the beautiful Olivia Langdon, lived in a fancy house, and hung out with high-class folk. But if Sam Clemens lived high on the hog, Mark Twain still wrote like a rabble-rousing resident of the Wild West out to defend the rights of ordinary Americans. And therein lay his success: People related to him, because he used their language (Twain was among the first writers to convey dialect in his writing), and wrote without pretense or affectation.

The Quotable Twain

"Familiarity breeds contempt—and babies."

"Golf is a good walk spoiled."

"Everything human is pathetic. The secret source of Humor itself is not joy but sorrow. There is no humor in heaven."

"Clothes make the man. Naked people have little or no influence in society."

"Everybody talks about the weather, but nobody ever does anything about it."

Twain remained funny throughout his life, but as his career progressed, his books—and his worldview—grew darker. Always somewhat irreverent, Twain became hostile to religion—and after his wife's death in 1903, he grew even more pessimistic. But even in his despair, Twain remained the kind of funny you can only be when you aren't kidding: As he wrote in *The Mysterious Stranger*, his unfinished last novel, "Against the assault of laughter nothing can stand."

GREAT SAVANTS IN HISTORY

Blind Tom Wiggins (1849–1908)

Probably the greatest autistic savant of the 19th century, "Blind" Tom Wiggins was born a slave and while still an infant was sold to the plantation of one James N. Bethune. Blind from birth, Wiggins learned to play the piano before he could speak. Bethune encouraged the boy, and although Wiggins's vocabulary reportedly never extended beyond 100 words, he could play any piece of music after hearing it just once. And once he'd played it a single time, it seems he memorized it forever: If he heard the first notes of the song, he would play it through. As a child, Wiggins played for everyone from President James Buchanan to Mark Twain, who was mightily impressed with the piano prodigy, saying that his music "swept [the audience] like a storm." For decades, Wiggins toured the world with Bethune, playing packed concert halls.

Bethune treated his prodigy well—particularly after the Civil War—but never gave Tom a significant portion of the $750,000 he'd earned. And in that sense, Wiggins remained a slave long after Emancipation. In fact, he is often called "America's last slave," since he was only released to his mother by federal court order in 1887. But in some ways, Wiggins fared better under the care of Bethune than he did afterwards, when his mother allowed him to live with an unscrupulous business-woman. Wiggins was still famous and widely popular when he died of a stroke at the age of 59.

Daniel Tammet (1979–)

A British savant whose autism affects his social skills in only very limited ways (which is to say that, like most math fanatics, he's a tad nerdy), Daniel Tammet knows a lot about pi. In fact, he once recited pi to the 22,514th digit in one five-hour period. And no, it wasn't an open-book test.

Neurologists are fascinated by Tammet in part because he has a neurological condition known as synaesthesia, wherein certain senses get a bit cross-eyed. People with synaesthesia may associate words with tastes, for instance, or sounds with colors. Tammet asserts that in his mind, each number up to 10,000 has a unique shape and feel, which is how he's able to remember such long strings of digits. He also claims he just *knows* instantly whether or not a particular number is prime.

All of which might sound a bit ridiculous, but consider this: Tammet can speak English, German, French, and Estonian, among many other languages. He claimed, in fact, he could learn a language in a week. So a television documentary challenged him to learn notoriously complex Icelandic. Seven days later, Tammet appeared on a live Icelandic talk show gabbing comfortably with the hosts.

One Non-Autistic Savant

Before Dustin Hoffman was Rain Man, Kim Peek (1951–) was. The inspiration for the Oscar-winning film, Peek was born with an enlarged head and some brain damage. And while he does have poor motor skills (for instance, he cannot button a shirt), and his social skills are limited, but they have improved with age—particularly since the movie *Rain Man* was released. Peek, however, *does not* have autism. In fact, he is extremely outgoing. And man, does he have a lot to talk about: Peek, who supposedly began memorizing books before he turned 2, can now recall more than 9,500 books from memory—which is easier when you read, as Peek does, about six pages per minute.

James Henry Pullen
(1835–1916)

Although autistic savants have a reputation for possessing a mild and benign genius, they're capable of profound aggression. Take for instance James Henry Pullen, the savant who is most famous for single-handedly building The Great Eastern, an immaculately constructed model ship that included 5,585 rivets and 13 detachable lifeboats. But ships weren't the only thing Pullen crafted: He once built a guillotine-esque contraption over the office door of a sanitarium employee he didn't like. Fortunately, the metal blade malfunctioned and didn't fall until after the staff member was safely through the doorway.

VOCAB FOR GENIUSES: UNCOMMON WORDS WORTH KNOWING

The noun **abligurition** (ab-lig-yoo-RISH-un) means spending an excessive amount of money on food. One historical figure who certainly engaged in this was Roman Emperor Vitellius, who, according to Roman historians, once ate 1,000 oysters in a single day, and also enjoyed huge platters of such delicacies as ostrich brain, flamingo tongue, and moray eel spleen.

If you want to point out someone's double chin but don't want to waste two words to do so, go with **choller** (CHAH-ler), which can also mean the hanging lip of a hound dog.

Euonym (YOO-oh-nim) is a noun meaning "a well-suited name." This is a particularly useful word for those awkward moments just after you greet your acquaintance Paul by saying, "Hey, Joe." You need only explain that Joe is Paul's euonym; "I mean, you just *look* like a Joe; there's something undeniably Joe-ish about you."

Of course, some people already have euonyms: The creator of the Hyde Park Miniature Museum is named DD Smalley, and it's hard to imagine a better suited name for a writer than the one Francine Prose was born with. But our favorite example of a euonym comes from the memoirist Amy Krouse Rosenthal, whose fourth grade teacher was named Mrs. Gotchalk.

Sitzpinkler

This isn't technically an English word yet, but we're working to change that. After all, such wonderful English words as *croissant* and *schadenfreude* and *Cheez Whiz* came into the popular vernacular relatively recently—and we believe **sitzpinkler** may be next in line. The German word that proves once and for all that the Germans have a word for everything, *sitzpinkler* means "a man who sits to urinate," although these days it is primarily used in Germany as a synonym for "wimp."

Wealthy ancient Greeks often paid mourners to show up at funerals of loved ones and weep vociferously. (You may recall from earlier in this very book that the poet Virgil hired mourners to weep at the funeral of his pet housefly.)

Believe it or not, there's actually a word for that career: Hired mourners are known as **moirologists** (moy-RAH-lih-jists).

Speaking of unusual jobs you didn't know justified their own terms, a **dactylio-glyph** (dack-TILL-ee-uh-gliff) is a person who engraves finger rings.

Ollendorffian (ah-lun-DORF-ee-un) is a brilliantly precise adjective: It means "written in the artificial and overly formal style of foreign-language phrase books," and is derived from the name of German grammarian Heinrich Ollendorff. The most aggressively Ollendorffian phrase we learned in French class was, "I am going to the library with my acquaintance Robert who works as an acrobat." Another fine example, from Erin McKean's *Weird and Wonderful Words*, is "Unhand me, Sir, for my husband, who is an Australian, awaits without."

The word **quark** (KWORK) is a noun meaning the subatomic elementary particles that are the basic building blocks of matter. Turns out that the physicist Murray Gell-Mann, who first proposed the name, was a big fan of James Joyce's notoriously difficult *Finnegan's Wake*. A poem in *Finnegan's Wake* includes the line "Three quarks for Muster Mark!" Gell-Mann picked *quark* mostly because he liked the sound of the word, and also because at the time physicists believed there were only three kinds of quarks (they now believe there are six).

The noun **gloze** (GLOZE) means a little note in the margin of text.

We Have a Particularly Hard Time with "Free Fallin'"

There's actually a word for the phenomenon where a song gets stuck in your head: Such a song is an **earworm**. A study conducted by a professor at the University of Cincinnati found that the theme from *Gilligan's Island* and "It's a Small World After All" were among the earwormiest songs on the planet. *It's a world of laughter, a world of something / It's a world of hmm and a world of mmm.* Wait. Where were we? Oh, right. Researchers hypothesize that one of the reasons earworms stick in our heads is that we're trying to fill in the blanks—either the notes don't resolve satisfactorily, or we don't quite remember the rhymes. Our brains want to bring closure to the song and so they repeat it over and over again, looking for the resolution. Other times, earworms are catchy, repetitive songs we liked in our youth but slowly grew to despise (see headline), which come back as ghouls to haunt our long-term memories.

Pop quiz: What do Bill Clinton, Pol Pot, Marie Curie, Oprah Winfrey, and Albert Einstein have in common? A. They are all **singletons**, the word meaning "people who are *not* conjoined twins."

Theoplasm (THEE-oh-plaz-m) is a noun meaning the material out of which gods are made. Related word: **ectoplasm** (EK-toh-plaz-m), a layer of fluid in cells, unless you are watching *Ghostbusters*, in which case it's the stuff ghosts are made out of.

WHAT GENIUSES KNOW ABOUT EVOLUTION

Among scientists, at least, evolution hasn't been controversial for a long time. Natural selection as a tool to propel and diversify life made sense to many biologists from the moment it was proposed, largely because Charles Darwin's 1859 book *On the Origin of Species* was so well-argued, and so meticulously detailed in its observations. (Darwin was rather obsessive-compulsive, after all—this is a guy who devoted eight years of his life to becoming the world's foremost authority on barnacles.) But for an idea that's been around for nearly 150 years, evolution continues to be the subject of extraordinarily contentious debate.

Most of us have a basic understanding of natural selection. Darwin compared natural selection to the way farmers breed livestock: In the past century, for example, the average chicken breast has drastically increased in size. This is partly due to hormones and feeding patterns, but also due to physical changes in the chickens themselves, because they are selectively bred to be bigger. That's artificial selection, but in the wild things work the same way: Those who develop advantageous changes tend to reproduce more. Scientists agree that over extended periods of time, natural selection has led to the diversification of life on earth. Indeed, the theory of natural

185

Some Interesting Facts About Darwin

Fact 1: Throughout his adult life, and for reasons that no one has ever understood, Darwin puked a lot. Must have been fun having him onboard the H.M.S. *Beagle*.

Fact 2: Charles Darwin was inspired to a life of science by his jack-of-all-intellectual-trades grandfather, Erasmus Darwin, who was famously plump. Erasmus was so obese, in fact, that he had to cut a semicircle out of his dining room table to make room for his belly.

Fact 3: Darwin's *other* grandfather was Josiah Wedgwood, of Wedgwood pottery fame.

selection helps us understand everything from bacterial antibiotic resistance to the slight differences between birds on different islands in the Galápagos.

Much of the most promising recent evolutionary research suggests that evolution may not be all about genetic mutations, however. Indeed, beneficial genetic mutations are exceedingly rare, at least these days—you see a lot more people with malignant mutations, like, say, cystic fibrosis, than you do people with awesome mutations, like, say, X-ray vision. Many evolutionary biologists believe that it isn't merely a question of random changes to a gene; the real magic of evolution may take place in how that gene is regulated—whether it is turned on or off, and how many proteins it encodes. Amazingly enough, these biological "switches" may ultimately prove even more vital to the evolutionary adaptations than the genes themselves.

Common Descent

The Theory of Universal Common Descent states that all organisms on earth descend from a single common ancestor—in essence, that if you just go back a few billion generations, human beings are kissing cousins to the bacteria *E. coli* (Note: You should not kiss *E. coli*.). In Darwin's day, the main justification for this theory was based on exterior observations—that, for instance, all birds have wings, even though many birds do not fly. Today, however, there's compelling genetic evidence for the theory: All cells, for instance, use nucleic acid as genetic material, and there are commonalities between the genetic code of all organisms—from people to roundworms. So when did this common ancestor live? Well, if being a single-celled puddle of nucleic acid can be called "living," about 3 billion years ago.

25 ISMS TO KNOW

Animism—usually used to mean the belief that ordinary, non-sentient objects are endowed with souls. See, for instance, *The Velveteen Rabbit*.

Antidisestablishmentarianism—with its 28 letters, it's the longest word commonly used in English—although, fair enough, it isn't *that* commonly used these days, since it refers to a 19th century movement to keep the Anglican Church as the official church of England. (The movement succeeded in England, but failed in Wales and elsewhere).

Baptism—an ism that's an act, not a belief, a baptism is a ritual of purification and rebirth. Baptism by water is practiced by Christians and Sikhs. In fact, the Christian version is actually rooted in the Jewish ritual of *mikvah*, a ritual bath that, these days, is used primarily by religious Jewish women post-menstruation.

Bilateralism—the term for relations between only two sovereign states, as opposed to the multilateralism that prevails today thanks to organizations like the United Nations and the G-8.

Cynicism—originally an ism that referred to an ancient Greek school of philosophy, which was actually not very cynical in the way we think of the word today. Ancient cynics believed in letting out their animalistic desires and acting however they felt—not in sitting around smoking clove cigarettes and dismissing all of life as a charade.

Deconstructionism—a school of analysis founded by Jacques Derrida, who sought to understand the manners in which authors construct meanings in their texts. And to understand the constructions, of course, you must deconstruct them.

Determinism—the philosophical belief that everything results from a chain of previous occurrences, that every effect has a cause, and therefore there's no such thing as a random event.

Embolism—a noun describing a blockage in a blood vessel. Of all the known isms, this is the one you least want to encounter personally. Pulmonary embolisms, in particular, can be fatal.

Existentialism—while it's no embolism, can be pretty uncomfortable, too. A philosophy marked by anxiety, isolation, and awareness of the impending and everlasting doom that is death, existentialism may not be the most entertaining philosophy on the market (that would be HappyHappyFunTimesism), but it makes for some great and provocative writing (Soren Kierkegaard, Albert Camus, Jean-Paul Sartre).

Fauvism—a brief but influential school of color-happy, early modern art. The name *les fauves*, which means "wild beasts," was originally intended to be disparaging, but with Fauvists including the likes of Paul Gauguin, Gustave Moureau, and Henri Matisse—the name eventually became pretty cool.

Gigantism—a real physical condition, which Yao Min doesn't suffer from. Although most humans taller than 7 feet got that way thanks to genetics and eatin' right, a few suffer from pituitary gigantism, an excess secretion of growth hormone that results in—well, becoming gigantic. Famous people who suffered from pituitary gigantism include Andre "The Giant" Roussimoff and Martin Van Buren Bates (who also incidentally suffered from Being-Named-After-a-Very-Mediocre-President-itis). Bates, who was nearly 8 feet tall, fought for the Confederate army in the Civil War before traveling the world with a circus.

Gnosticism—any number of belief systems—including many early Christian sects—that focused on gnosis, i.e., mystical knowledge of God.

Hedonism and gnosticism would only end up near each other in an alphabetical list, since gnostics rarely indulged in the pure sensual pleasures of the hedonist. Hedonism means seeking pleasure—and nothing else.

Heliocentrism—the belief that the sun (*helios*) is at the center of the solar system, and not the earth. Believe it or not, there are still those who argue that the universe revolves around a stationary earth—that belief is now known as modern geocentrism, although we can't for the life of us figure out what's so modern about it.

Ism—a word on its own, incidentally (you can even play it in Scrabble). Generally used to mean "an ideology."

Jingoism—the belief that if you walk loudly and carry a big stick, and if you frequently hit people with that big stick, your country will come out on top. The term, meaning "extreme nationalism marked by an aggressive and hostile foreign policy," originated in an 1878 British pub song: *We don't want to fight / But by jingo, if we do / We've got the ships / We've got the men / We've got the money, too.*

Narcissism—the belief—You know what, could we just interrupt this whole book for a minute and talk about how good looking the **mental_floss** staff is? There's no doubt we're the hottest, most fascinating nerds since Melissa Joan Hart*.

Onanism—a synonym for masturbation. It was particularly popular (the word, we mean—not the act itself) until the late 19th century, and in fact one of Mark Twain's funniest speeches was 1879's "On the Science of Onanism." It concluded, "If you must gamble your lives sexually, don't play a lone hand too much." That kind of double entendre kept the speech from being published until 1943.

Pointilism—a painting style made famous by the likes of Georges Seurat and Paul Signac. Pointilism uses small dots of paint and highly contrasting colors to create a neoimpressionist effect.

Romanticism—a broad artistic and intellectual movement that, in response to the rationalism (there's another one!) of the Enlightenment, emphasized strong emotion and the importance of individual feeling. Romantic poets included Percy Bysshe Shelley, John Keats, and William Wordsworth; Romantic composers included Mozart and Haydn; and Romantic comedians include Julia Roberts, Hugh Grant, and more and more, one John Cusack.

Spoonerism—word games in which consonants are switched around. Named after the Reverend William Spooner, who was notoriously prone to accidental Spoonerisms from the pulpit. He once noted, for instance, that "The Lord is a shoving leopard," and that, "It is kisstomary to cuss the bride." Damn you, bride!

---

* who really is a nerd. She has memorized the first 300 digits of pi just for fun.

Transubstantiationism (which we dare you to say five times fast)—the belief that during the Eucharist, the bread and wine at the altar really become the body and blood of Christ. This is one of the central disagreements between Catholics and Protestants, who might be said to espouse antitransubstantiationism.

Ultramontanism—sounds like it ought to be the belief that Montana is really, really awesome, but it's actually the argument that the authority of the Pope (who lives *ultra montes*, over the mountains of the Alps) supersedes local authority.

Utilitarianism—the ethical theory that seeks the greatest good for the greatest number, which sounds like an excellent idea, although it has been used to justify radical political movements on both ends of the spectrum, from fascism to communism.

Zionism—the movement that worked to create a homeland for Jewish people, which culminated with the establishment of Israel in 1948. Speaking of noted Zionists...

YOUR MODEL
SCIENCE GENIUS:
ALBERT EINSTEIN

We can think of no better example of genius to leave you with than Albert Einstein. The biggest brain in science since at least Isaac Newton was born in 1879. The son of a German feather-bed salesman, Einstein grew up in a Jewish family that was so distinctly nonobservant that he actually attended *Catholic* school. Even in his youth, Einstein was truly a citizen of the world—he spent time in Italy and Switzerland, and he was just 17 when he renounced his German citizenship and became a "stateless individual."

Stateless, and a little shiftless, too. Although he published his first scientific paper when he was 21—it was about capillary forces in drinking straws, and in it he (seriously) tried to use drinking straws to unify all the laws of physics—Einstein had trouble finding a worthwhile teaching gig. By 1902, Einstein was working at the Swiss patent office. And then, in 1905, while still approving patents for the Swiss versions of lava lamps and Dixie cups, Einstein published four papers that were so important that 1905 has forever since been known as Einstein's *annus mirabilis*—his year of wonders.

1. "On a Heuristic Viewpoint Concerning the Production and Transformation of Light" proposed that light is absorbed and emitted in discrete packets, which Einstein called quanta. Each quantum exists at a point in space at any given time. This paper proposed the idea, now readily accepted, that light acts as both a particle and a wave.

2. With his next paper, Einstein once and for all established the actual existence of atoms by showing how tiny particles inside a liquid move around randomly (the phenomenon is known as Brownian Motion, after a guy named Brown and not because the particles are any particular color).

3. His third paper proposed special relativity, which proved the speed of light was fixed no matter the speed of the observer, and in doing so turned Newtonian physics on its head.

4. Einstein's final paper, "Does the Inertia of a Body Depend Upon Its Energy Content?" established, well, that the inertia of a body depends upon its energy content. It was this paper that contained his famous equation $E = mc^2$ (where E = energy, m = mass, and c = the speed of light, which is about 186,282 miles per second).

In retrospect, all four of these papers could have justified their own Nobel Prizes—although Einstein only won once, and it was 16 years after his *annus mirabilis*. World famous by 1920, Einstein moved to America in 1932, and he remained in Princeton, New Jersey, for the rest of his life. Much of his later career was devoted to the ultimately fruitless search for what he called

A Model Genius, But Not a Saint

Einstein was pretty great: He helped found the International Rescue Committee to help opponents of Hitler living in Europe. He loved Gandhi ("I believe Gandhi's views were the most enlightened of all political men of our time"). And he was involved in the American Civil Rights movement for decades—he once called racism "America's greatest disease," and risked his reputation to testify on behalf of W.E.B. Du Bois when Du Bois was baselessly accused of being a communist spy.

But he wasn't perfect. And if you don't believe us, just ask Einstein's poor first wife, Mileva. As Einstein put it in a letter to his mistress (and cousin!) Elsa, "I treat my wife as an employee I cannot fire." He might have genuinely meant *employee*—some have speculated that Mileva helped Einstein develop the theory of special relativity (his letters to her refer to "our" work on relativity). Most scholars believe, though, that relativity was Einstein's work alone. Regardless, he *did* eventually fire Mileva (they divorced in 1919), replacing her with the aforementioned cousin Elsa.

a "generalized theory of gravitation," a single elegant expression of how all the fundamental forces in the universe function. He may not have succeeded in that final goal, but it may be centuries before we again see anyone as scientifically deft and creative as Einstein. Well, except *you*, of course.

Congratulations! You are now a Genius.

Whew. It was a long, hard slog. But you made it. And just look at you now! You appear physiologically similar to your former self, only now you understand string theory, macroeconomics, and find it impossible to forget the troubling fact that Ernest Hemingway's mom dressed him in girls' clothes.

We've done our part. Now you have to do yours. And to that end, we've constructed this handy list of Fertile Fields You Can Now Till:

Physics

- It would be nice if someone would go ahead and invent a Theory of Everything that explained all the major laws governing the universe. As previously noted, string theory seems to be leading us in the right direction, but a solid push from a genius could be very helpful right now.

- Is the universe expanding? Or contracting? Or just spinning? And is this the only universe? Definitively answering just one of these questions will likely mean that you have invented a pretty incredible telescope. It should also land you one of them fancy Nobel Prize things.

Biology

- Figure out the exact purpose of the long stretches of so-called "junk DNA" found in the genomes of pretty much every organism, from wolves to Wolf Blitzer.

- Cure cancer. Go on—do it. Honestly, don't even finish the book. Just go to the laboratory—what, you don't have a laboratory? Okay, get one. We'll wait. Ready? Good. Now, go to the laboratory and cure cancer. If you need a little hint to get you started: gene therapy.

Philosophy

- Do we have free will? If you have an answer, and can prove it, you could be the Next Great American Philosopher. Which, incidentally, would make an excellent reality show.

Music

- This is a somewhat tough field to break into on account of how it already contains so many geniuses—Philip Glass, Avril Lavigne, etc. But one way to make a significant impact to the world of contemporary popular music is to invent a new subgenre. To that end, you'll need to tweak—ever so slightly—the basic musical format of a current subgenre. That should be easy enough, but here's where the genius comes in: You need a name. We suggest something that sounds like it could be a word but isn't. Recent examples include *crunk* and *emo*.

Arts + Literature

- It's been a number of years since we had a good old-fashioned influential art movement. You know, like your Dadaists, Cubists, Fauvists, Impressionists, and Pop Artists. All you need is a catchy name, some convoluted art theory, and—here's the tricky part—a fresh and compelling approach to art.

Politics

- You know what would be immensely helpful, although admittedly it will take a sizable genius? Ending war. Don't despair just because it seems like a lofty goal: What if Gandhi had quit when he saw the immensity of the task before him? Then Ben Kingsley probably never would have won an Oscar! D'you ever think about that?!

So, there's your list, Geniuses. Go out there and knock 'em dead, already!

ABOUT THE
EDITORS

Will Pearson and *Mangesh Hattikudur* met as freshmen at Duke University, and in their senior year parlayed their cafeteria conversations into the first issue of **mental_floss** magazine. Five years later, they're well on their way to creating a knowledge empire. In addition to the magazine, a board game, and a weekly *CNN Headline News* segment, the two have also collaborated on seven **mental_floss** books. In their spare time, Will and Mangesh also tour the country performing folk music under the name Peter, Paul, and Mary.

John Green is the author of the award-winning novel *Looking for Alaska* (2005), which has been translated into eight languages and is being made into a film by Paramount Pictures. John also contributes commentary to NPR's *All Things Considered*, and works for *Booklist* magazine, reviewing literary fiction and children's picture books, as well as pretty much everything that gets published involving boxing, conjoined twins, and/or little people (although John himself is quite tall). In short, he's the closest thing the **mental_floss** staff has to being a genius.

© Thomas Balsamo

Autism is heartbreaking
But it's not hopeless.

Most people take smiling, talking and laughing for granted - simply part of being human. But for the more than one million Americans affected by autism, these simple human experiences are extremely difficult or nonexistent.

Autism is a neuro-developmental disorder that impairs, often severely, an individual's ability to communicate and interact with others. This impairment creates a world of isolation and frustration for even the sweetest and smartest of souls. Autism is painful and heartbreaking, but it's not hopeless.

At Cure Autism Now, we're accelerating scientific research to treat and cure autism. We believe in urgency, excellence in science, collaboration and open access to information. To learn more about our innovative research programs and how you can help, call us or visit us online.

888.8.AUTISM

www.cureautismnow.org

A Genius for Every Occasion . . .

mental_floss Cocktail Party Cheat Sheets
0-06-088251-4 (paperback)
Available 6/06

Don't be a wallflower at your next social outing, just fake your way through the conversation! These cheat sheets will have you equipped to handle the brainiest of topics in no time.

mental_floss Scatterbrained
0-06-088250-6 (paperback)
Available 7/06

Based on *mental_floss* magazine's popular "Scatterbrained" section, this book features thousands of juicy facts and tantalizing bits of trivia that are connected humorously—from Greece (the country) to *Grease* (the movie) to greasy foods and on and on.

mental_floss What's the Difference?
0-06-088249-2 (paperback)
Available 7/06

Want to spot a Monet from a Manet, kung fu from karate, or Venus from Serena Williams? Piece of cake! Whether you're trying to impress your boss, mother-in-law, attractive singles, or your 4th grade teacher, *mental_floss* has hundreds of quick tricks to make you sound like a genius.

mental_floss Genius Instruction Manual
0-06-088253-0 (paperback)
Available 11/06

The *Genius Instruction Manual* is the ultimate crash course on how to talk, act, and even dress like a genius. Presented by the brainiac team at *mental_floss*, it's the one-stop shop for today's impossibly clever, cultured, and sophisticated person.

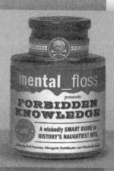

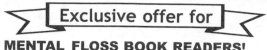